The Secret Life of Trees

By: Robin Blackwell

Cover art by Dimitrievna

Other works by Robin Blackwell:

Devotee of War
The Prince's Sacrifice
The Well

Chapter One: Let's Talk About the Tree

Who did Emma think she was fooling, anyway?

I'd had that room long before she had. Did she think I didn't know that the tree was at the perfect height to climb down and sneak out of the house after curfew? Please. I'd been doing that since before she was old enough to realize that two plus two equals four.

So yes, when she started showing up to the breakfast table with shadows under her eyes and when I started getting reports that she was sleeping through her classes, it was pretty obvious what was going on. I'm not an idiot.

But I waited. I wanted to give her a chance to come to me, because honestly this whole thing was new for both of us. She'd only been out of her coma for a year, and she'd only just stopped her physical therapy. I didn't want to crack the whip too hard, but if she was falling asleep in class than she was staying out too late. I tried dropping hints, asking her things like whether she was staying up too late doing homework or something, and she never gave me an honest answer. So then I got a bit more direct and asked her who she was going out with every night. That earned me a glare and a very cold, "Nobody." I hadn't realized that my sister had that kind of look in her, actually.

And then there was the increasing crime all over the neighborhood. We grew up in a quiet little town, but lately things seemed to be somewhat less than quiet. And by somewhat less than quiet, I meant that there were more murders now than there had been, as opposed to just petty theft.

A month after the first teacher had called home, and the day that the fourth teacher did so, I couldn't let it go any longer. I sat her down in the kitchen over dinner. Normally we ate in front of the TV, so she definitely knew something was up. She probably even suspected what it was, given the look on my face and the look on her own.

"Let's talk about the tree," I said.

Her glare was, arguably, one of the most intense glares I'd gotten from her yet. Her green eyes looked like they were about to shoot sparks at me. "What about it?" she asked, in a voice that probably could have frozen lava.

"You're using it every night," I said. I smiled at her when her glare ratcheted up another level. "Come on, Emma, I'm just trying to-"

"Trying to what?" She laughed. "Be my father? You aren't. Cut the tree down and I'll find another way to get out at night."

I flinched. "Right." I took a deep breath and let it out slowly and tried not to show how much her words cut me. I wasn't her father. That was true. She was my sister, not my daughter. That didn't mean I didn't want what was best for her. "I don't want you going out anymore."

"Or you'll what?" She stared at me, defiance clear in the stubborn set of her chin. I knew that look well, because I'd worn it for much of my life.

"Or there will have to be repercussions," I said. I didn't break her gaze. She wanted to play hardball with me? I didn't want to play with her, but that didn't mean I didn't understand the rules of the game. I'd been a teenager once too, and it hadn't even been that long ago.

"Ooh, are you going to tell me I can't go out? Like I'm already doing every night without your permission?" Emma laughed. It was a bitter, broken thing, like shards of glass exploding from her throat.

The sound cut much like glass might have and I stared down at my plate of untouched food. "Emma, please, I'm just…" I stopped and took a deep breath. "You're my sister. You know I want the world for you. What happened to your plans for Yale?"

Emma looked away. "It's not like my grades are dropping." Her jawline softened, though, and her eyes grew a bit moist. "I'm sorry, Jamie, I know you're trying too." She sniffled.

I broke. "I know this isn't easy on you, Ems," I said. I stood and stepped around the table, going to her side. She buried her face in my stomach and clung to me, her fingers clutching at the back of my shirt. "We're gonna get through this, though."

"Course we are," she said, sniffling. "We're Gardners. We get through anything." Still, she clung to me.

I wondered if this was grief at the loss of our parents or if it was something else. If, in her grief, she'd gotten herself into something she couldn't get out of. Maybe that was the problem? Maybe… ha. Maybe I was in over my head. "Listen, Ems, I think maybe you should start seeing someone," I said hesitantly.

I saw someone, after all. Gabrielle was a lifesaver. She kept me grounded in all of the madness following the car accident, when I hadn't even known if Emma would live or not. She helped me when I was figuring out how to break the news to Emma that not only had Mom and Dad died, but they'd been buried while she was in her coma.

"See someone?" Emma started to laugh. She pulled away and buried her head in her arms, her shoulders heaving with her laughter.

That was sort of offensive, actually. She knew I saw Gabrielle every week. "What's so funny about that thought?" I asked, my hurt echoing through my voice.

Immediately her laughter cut off. "No, Jamie, it's not that, it's just that I wouldn't even know where to start!" She stared at me, her eyes wide with apology. "I just… I really miss them, you know? And I've been having a lot of trouble sleeping, and I just… sometimes it's easier to go for a walk than to try and sleep, you know?"

I did know, actually. "I get it," I said with a sigh. And what could I even say to that? Don't go for walks, just try to sleep? That didn't seem like it would help at all. "You know, a therapist could help with that. Gabrielle's full, and there'd be that whole conflict of interest thing, but there are a few others in her office that could probably take you on."

She shook her head. "Thanks, Jamie, but I think I'll be okay." She smiled at me. I'd never seen a more insincere expression on her face.

What could I do? Punishing her for grieving seemed like a terrible idea. I couldn't really force her to go to a therapist because Emma was stubborn enough that she probably wouldn't talk if I tried. "Okay," I said finally, and returned to my side of the table. "But you know, you could wake me next time. I miss them too."

I stayed awake most nights thinking about the last time I'd seen them. They'd been fine. To get the call a month later had been… well. It was the worst surprise of my life. The months after that had been pretty nightmarish too, trying to sort everything out with the funeral and the doctors and with Emma…

She was still smiling at me. "I'll do that," she said.

I think she forgot that I knew what she looked like when she lied because I'm the one who taught her to do it.

7

*   *   *

I didn't want to do it.

All teenage girls had their secrets, but not all teenage girls were climbing out of a tree in the middle of the night doing who knew what with who knew who in a town that was getting steadily more dangerous. And not all teenage girls were my little sister who'd already almost died once. I waited until she snuck out again, because of course she was going to, and I followed her.

It wasn't as hard as I'd thought it would be. I'd pretty much figured she'd be getting in a car and I'd have to follow her somehow without her realizing that it was my beat up old jeep trailing her. But no, she stayed on foot, and it was relatively easy to stick to the shadows. It didn't take me long before I realized that she was headed for the park three blocks away from us.

What the hell did she want there? It was the park where we'd played together as kids, and our parents had taken us there frequently, but we literally hadn't been there for years. Not since I'd gone off to college ten years ago. Maybe Emma had continued to go with our parents? She'd only been five, after all...

But no, I was wrong. We didn't stop at the park. We kept going. Deeper into town, actually, until we were downtown and wandering the quiet streets. She hadn't noticed me yet, which was something of a miracle. Also concerning, because

I was pretty sure I wasn't being subtle. Why hadn't she noticed me? Maybe she was sleepwalking?

"I told her that you wouldn't stay away forever," someone said beside me.

I froze. Then I turned my head to the left and found myself staring at the most beautiful and strangest man I'd ever seen. His hair was long and wild and many shades of green. His skin was dark brown and patterned like tree bark. He was staring at me with sharp golden eyes without so much as a smile on his face.

"Sorry?" I squeaked. Then I blushed, embarrassed, because that sound was awful and I hadn't realized that I could actually make it.

"Emma. I warned her that you'd catch on and she should probably just tell you. Also, you could be helping her." He sounded almost bored as he stared after my sister, who'd continued on her way. I'd lost sight of her now.

"Sorry, but who are you?"

He looked at me like I was an idiot. There really aren't words for the amount of disdain in his voice when he said, "I can't imagine that anyone is as foolish as you."

"Wow," I said, drawing the word out. "And here I was just thinking that I couldn't imagine anyone as rude as you."

The... tree? Whatever, glared at me. "Rude?" He laughed. "Please. I'm not the one who climbed all over someone for years without so much as a please or a thank you."

I opened my mouth to retort but closed it with a snap. "Huh?" I finally asked.

He rolled his eyes. "I'm the spirit of the tree in your yard, you moron. You may call me Leaf, since your useless human tongues can't pronounce my proper name."

"You're a... tree spirit?" Was that a thing? When had that become a thing? Maybe I'd been hit by a car while I was trying to follow Emma and this was all a weird dream. That was the only thing that would make sense right about now, because tree spirit certainly wasn't adding up.

"Your father didn't tell you either, I see." Leaf sighed, a great heaving noise that sounded curiously like wind tearing through the branches of a tree. "She's a Gardener."

"Gardner," I said, automatically correcting the pronunciation of our last name. It was a pretty common problem, actually.

Leaf sighed that same heavy sigh once more. "Gardener," he said flatly. "You... ugh. It's easier to show you. Come along, James." He started walking and, since I didn't really have any other choice because I still needed to catch up to Emma, I followed him.

We didn't go far. Just around a few corners until we were standing in a dark alley. And there was Emma, glowing with this soft green light, facing off against something that looked similar to Leaf but seemed angrier. Meaner. Bigger, too, much bigger. It was snarling at Emma, its words unintelligible. I could feel something strange coming from it, something dark and twisted and angry.

Vines began to grow around Emma, snaking around her legs. She danced away from them, breaking their tenuous hold. She didn't seem at all concerned, and she began to chant in a language I'd never heard before and certainly couldn't identify. Her fingers moved in time with her words and the green light surrounding her began to surround the thing snarling at her.

It… calmed, I guess, was the only word for it. The snarling faded and in the end there was a tiny little thing, maybe half of Emma's size, staring up her with the sweetest expression on its face. It melted into the ground and Emma dropped to her knees, her breath coming in harsh pants.

I went to step forward, to help her to her feet or ask her what was going on or something, but I couldn't move. Leaf was holding onto my wrist. "Come on," he said shortly. "She doesn't want you here. Says you have enough on your plate without this."

His grip was too strong for me to break, and when he began to drag me away I had no choice but to stumble after him. "Are you out of your fucking mind?" I snarled to him even as I tried to pull away. "That's my sister back there, sitting on the filthy floor of some alley, and you're telling me I can't go help her?"

"I'm telling you that your sister's already pretty worried about you and if you want to make that worse you're welcome to go back there and let her know that you saw her tonight," Leaf said. He released me and gestured back in the direction we'd come.

"I…" I stopped. I didn't want to make things worse for her. Emma already had so much on her plate and I didn't want to add to it. "Right," I said, because what else could I do. "How do I help her, then?"

Leaf smiled at me, like I'd finally done something right. "Well. There are options. If you're interested, and if you think you're up to the challenge."

I didn't know if I was, but I would be damned if I was going to let my little sister face whatever this stuff was on her own. "I'm up for it," I said, with more confidence than I felt.

"Good. Then come see me tomorrow while your sister is at school." Leaf started to walk away from me.

"Wait!" I cried before realizing that I already knew the answer to my question. Then winced when he turned to look at me with an inquiring expression on his peculiar face. "I was going to ask you where I could find you, but I think I've got it figured out."

He laughed at me. "My tree, of course." Then he was gone, dissolving like leaves blowing away in the wind. It was a disconcerting image to say the least.

And now I was standing alone on a sidewalk in the middle of town with a long walk home ahead of me and no idea what was going on. Great. Lovely. Hopefully I wouldn't run into Emma on the way. Or maybe I would, and I could make her explain in spite of what Leaf had suggested.

Or maybe I wouldn't.

I sighed and started walking and hoped that everything would seem clearer once I'd gotten home. Or once I'd slept on it, if I could even get to sleep. It probably wouldn't.

Chapter Two: A Meeting with a Tree

Sleep wasn't a thing that happened for me that night. I know, I know, I'm shocked too.

I tried, but I just kept tossing and turning. Finally, about around the time the sun was going to rise, I gave up on the notion of sleep entirely and headed downstairs. I would make a kick ass breakfast for Emma, then maybe get some sleep before trying to talk to the tree.

God. My life.

Cooking was... soothing. I heated up the oven and threw in a can of cinnamon rolls, then started mixing up a quiche. By the time Emma tripped her way down the stairs at 6:30, both the quiche and the cinnamon rolls were ready, as were both bacon and sausage, and some freshly squeezed orange juice. Her eyebrows went up, then down at the sight of the food on the table.

"Couldn't sleep?" She slid into a seat and stared at me expectantly.

"Rough night," I said agreeably, and handed her a plate of food. "So eat up, because there's no way I can eat all of this alone."

She laughed. "No, guess not." She took a bite of the quiche, then her eyes widened and she was shoving it into her mouth. "Damn, Jamie, you need to cook like this more often."

I grinned. "Really? Because I wouldn't want you to gain any-" I cut off when she chucked a cinnamon roll at my head. I caught it and took a gleeful bite of it. "What a way to waste food," I chided her.

"Oh, fuck you," she muttered through a full mouth. "Has anyone ever told you that you're an asshole sometimes?"

"You, numerous times," I said. I took a bite after I was finished eating and sighed. Fucking delicious. She was right, I really should cook like this more often. Especially since it was relaxing, and lately I hadn't really done much in the way of relaxing.

"Rude." Then she laughed, a bright sound that I hadn't heard nearly often enough in the past few months. "Jamie, you're the best, you know that?"

I opened my mouth to say something, anything, about how if I was the best she could talk to me and come to me with anything and then I realized it wouldn't do any good. She knew that. She just… didn't want to talk to me about this thing she was doing late at night wandering the city all by herself. "I do know that, as it happens," I said with as much cheer as I could muster.

It worked, because she beamed at me. "Good." Then she finished eating and darted back upstairs to finish getting ready. She was out the door by seven o'clock and I was left sitting in the kitchen, staring at a table that was still mostly full of food.

I sighed and began the laborious process of cleaning up. It didn't take too long, and soon the food was put away and the last of the dishes were soaking in the sink. I looked outside at the tree and wondered how early was too early for a tree spirit, then decided that seven o'clock might not be early for him but it was for me and there was no way I could handle that so early in the morning.

I settled on the couch and flicked on the television instead of going outside. There wasn't much on, but after a while I flicked to a random channel and let the mind numbing show, whatever it was, soothe me to sleep.

I woke up only an hour or two later when the show had turned to some action movie with way too many explosions and not enough logic. I turned the television off and went into the kitchen. I finished the dishes, then turned to stare out at the tree. Was it still too early? Could I really deal with this?

Not before lunch. I headed to the office and stared at a blank computer screen for a few hours as I tried to decide what to do with the rest of my life. A common theme, and one that I still hadn't figured out yet. Things had... well, to say that they'd changed with Mom and Dad's death was an understatement. The money they'd left behind, and the money we'd received from the insurance company and the settlement with the other driver, they meant that I really didn't have to work for a long time. If ever. And Emma wouldn't need to either.

But still.

Sitting around the house all day staring at blank computer screens wasn't my idea of a good time. And it wasn't any way to spend the rest of my life. So I wanted to do something, but I hadn't figured out what yet.

I sighed, unlocked the computer, and wiled away a few hours playing solitaire and other stupid games. Then I went for lunch when my stomach growled, around one o'clock in the afternoon. And then I couldn't put it off any longer because Emma would be home soon enough and I should probably talk to the tree before she was.

I went out into the yard, a mug of coffee in my hand. There was the tree, same as it always was. In the yard, not moving, not doing anything interesting or anything. Just... there. Being a tree. "Hi there," I said to it, feeling like an idiot.

I got no response. I groaned. "Seriously? This is really hard for me already, the least you could do is not have been a hallucination or something last night."

Still nothing. Was I crazy? The possibility wasn't such a strange one. I could be crazy. I really, really didn't want to be crazy. "Please?" I tried.

There was a snort of laughter behind me and I turned. He was standing right there, his lips twisted into a smirk and his eyes lit up with amusement. "You're an adorable idiot, did you know that?"

"Well, I was just talking to a tree," I muttered. I rubbed at my neck and hoped that I didn't look as embarrassed as I felt. "Anyway. You wanted to talk to me today? Maybe explain some things about what I saw last night, because I'm still not entirely certain that I didn't just imagine everything."

"You didn't," Leaf said. He crossed over to settle on one of the roots of the tree and looked at me expectantly.

I sighed. This wasn't going to be a quick conversation. I'd known it wasn't, hence the coffee. I sat across from him, my legs folded. I leaned back against the tree trunk and tried to get comfortable. "Right. So talk, then."

"Such a gracious invitation," Leaf said, the sarcasm all but dripping from his voice. "However could I refuse?"

I glared at him and he laughed merrily. "Asshole," I muttered.

"I have been called such many times by many different people, your father included." Leaf had an almost fond expression on his face as he mentioned my father.

"You knew my father?" I asked.

"Of course I did," Leaf said, sounding almost offended. "Your father was a Gardner, wasn't he? The same as you and your sister. Your family has lived in this house, with my tree, for at least five generations. It was a tragedy when your father's mother died giving birth to him, ensuring that there would be no Gardener for his generation."

I took a deep breath and let it out slowly. "Because my father couldn't be a Gardener?" I guessed, even though I really had no idea.

He almost looked approving. "Exactly so. It's a matrilineal talent. Honestly, prior to the birth of your sister, I wasn't even aware that your father could even carry the talent. But when she was born, I knew." He smiled a bit. "She was such a bright baby."

"So this is something she was born with, and I wasn't, and that's why I have to let her go off and do her thing at night while I stay at home and worry about her?"

"Pretty much," Leaf said with a shrug.

"And how did she learn about this talent of hers, anyway?" I asked, my suspicion growing. Leaf knew an awful lot about this, after all.

"I told her, of course," he said calmly.

"Why?" I asked, my teeth gritted. That had looked dangerous last night. Why would he want my little sister to be in danger?

"Because..." He sighed. Then he looked at the tree we were sitting on. "Do you understand what I am?" he asked, his tone only the slightest bit condescending.

"A tree spirit," I said immediately. Because, assuming that I wasn't hallucinating everything, that was what Leaf was. The spirit of the tree that had lived in my backyard for the last hundred plus years.

"That's right," Leaf said. "I'm not the only one. There are millions of us. Or... there used to be. But humans... you develop. You destroy trees, and plants, and flowers, and you never think about what happens to the spirits of the things you destroy." He shuddered and shifted so that he was closer to the trunk of the tree.

"I'm not sure I understand." I didn't. This whole thing made no sense to me. I got that he was saying that we killed plants and that plants had spirits, but what did that have to do with my sister?

"Most of the time, when it's just grass or flowers, a plant doesn't have enough of a spirit to be dangerous. Oh, maybe if enough little spirits die they might be able to make a person sick, but for the most part the spirits of little things fade quietly away. It's the ones that don't fade with the loss of their home that are the dangerous ones."

I closed my eyes and let my head fall back against the trunk of the tree. "You're telling me that trees get angry when they die," I guessed. That sounded utterly ridiculous, and I hoped that Leaf was aware of how insane he sounded. How insane I probably sounded, even saying something like that out loud.

"That's what I'm saying," Leaf said. "Your sister is a Gardener, which means she can... prune the overgrowth away, if you will. Soothe the anger of the spirits and send them to their rest before they hurt anyone."

"You're trying to tell me that my sister is a superhero," I said, trying the words on for size. They didn't really feel right coming from my lips and I felt stupid saying them out loud. "She's not. She's a teenage girl."

"Well. She's never going to run around in spandex and Kevlar," Leaf said, a quiver of laughter in his voice. "But I suppose the comparison is an apt one. The most dangerous spirits are the angriest ones, the ones who have been either without a home for the longest or are freshly killed. And we have many spirits who have gone without homes for far too long because we haven't had a Gardener to soothe them."

"So this is dangerous, right?" I opened my eyes to glance at Leaf. He stared back at me, his gaze even. "You're asking me to let my sister go into danger."

"It is dangerous. Spirits can be... powerful." He glanced at his tree and shivered. "If I ever lost my tree I-" Then he cut off.

21

"You... what?"

"I would be incredibly dangerous," he said, his voice far away. Then he shook his head. "Forgive me. The thought is a painful one. Yes. This is dangerous. But your sister is well-equipped to deal with the dangerous nature of it."

"You told me last night that I might be able to help her, even if I don't have the talent for Gardening." My eyebrows lifted in challenge as I stared at him.

"So I did," Leaf said with a nod. "You... are sensitive to certain things. The emotions of those around you are often particularly taxing, are they not? Especially negative emotions?"

"I identify with people easily, if that's what you're asking." I looked away, a bit uncomfortable because I knew where this was going. I'd told a girlfriend once about my experiences with other people's emotions and she'd insisted that I had a Gift. Capital G required. We'd broken up pretty quickly after that. I mean, it hadn't been just that, there had been other things she'd wanted that I... didn't. But that had definitely been one of the two main causes.

"You're uncomfortable with this conversation," Leaf said, and stood. "Then we'll table this for now." He pressed himself against the tree and I just knew somehow that he was going to leave.

"Wait!" I cried, and jumped up. I grabbed his wrist. It was warm in my hand, and I don't know why that surprised me. I guess I'd expected my hand to pass through or his wrist to be cold since he wasn't really alive. That, more than anything, convinced me that I wasn't crazy.

He turned to me and glared down at my hand on his wrist. "I would thank you not to touch me," he said coldly.

"I'm sorry," I said quickly, and dropped my hand. "I just... I want to help my sister. I don't care if I'm uncomfortable."

He studied me, and never before had I been so closely scrutinized. "Okay," he said finally. "I see that you're sincere." He settled back down and I sat too, this time folding my legs under myself.

"Thank you," I said, and put all of the sincerity I could into the words.

There was a flicker of something in his gaze and his lips curled up. "You are an Empath. You can both feel what others feel and project emotions onto them, as you just did with me."

"Sorry," I said quickly. I hadn't meant to do that.

Leaf shook his head. "It's fine. It only proves that you are, in fact, capable of helping your sister. Some plants, you see, aren't dangerous at first. They have the potential to become terribly dangerous, but if someone were to help them along then they might fade without ever becoming a danger."

I stared at him. "You want me to be a plant therapist," I finally said.

He grinned. "In a sense, yes."

"I'm not even remotely qualified for that." I wasn't qualified for anything, actually, except writing really bad essays and turning them in a day after they were due, but that wasn't really the point.

"Fortunately, there's no board exam for you to pass," he said serenely. "Did you want to help your sister or not?"

"I do, of course I do!" I took a deep breath and said, "So I guess I'll give it a shot then."

"Excellent!" Leaf almost beamed at me. "I'm so pleased to hear you say that. I'll let you know when I have the first spirit for you to speak with." Then he glanced behind me and grinned.

"Jamie?" Emma asked from behind me.

I stood and turned and tried not to look guilty. "Hey, Ems. Back early from school?"

She stared at me. "It's three o'clock," she said slowly. "I'm actually a bit late because…" She cut herself off with a nervous little laugh. "I'm a bit late. What are you doing out here?" She crossed the yard and hugged me, and I could feel her gesturing frantically at Leaf behind my back.

Probably telling him to go away because she didn't realize that I could see the spirit, or that I'd just been having a conversation with him. Honestly. My life, a bad sitcom with superhero tendencies. Anyway.

"Just having some coffee," I said. I pulled away from her and lifted my cup to my lips and tried not to wince. It had gone cold, because of course it had.

"Outside?" Emma asked.

I shrugged. "Just communing with nature," I said innocently. "But if it's bothering you, I'll head inside."

When I left the yard, I heard her hissing rather noisily at Leaf, ordering him to stay away from me because if he got me involved something unfortunate might happen to his tree.

I whistled as I headed into the office, cheered by the thought of her being so angry on my behalf, and by the thought that I could maybe help her with her... task. Calling. God. Really? My sister shouldn't have a fucking calling. She should be worrying about her grades and getting into a good college.

I sighed and tried to hold onto my cheer. I could help her now that I knew, and that was the important thing.

Chapter Three: My First Plant

Later that day, over dinner, Emma fessed up to why she'd been late home. Detention, apparently, for falling asleep yet again in class.

I groaned and rubbed at my forehead. "Ems, I get that you're having trouble sleeping, but you've got to stop," I said.

She didn't say anything, but instead stared mutinously at her plate.

"Seriously, Ems," I said. She still didn't look at me. I tried another tactic. "They might not let me keep you if you keep falling asleep in class."

Her head jerked up and she stared at me. "What?" she asked, her voice breathy with surprise.

"You have to know that they didn't really want me to have you in the first place. I'm... too young. Aunt Elise and Uncle Barry were better choices, from their perspectives."

Emma wrinkled her nose. "Uncle Barry just wanted the money, though," she said. She stirred her food on her plate but didn't actually lift any of it to her lips. The shadows under her eyes looked like bruises, they were getting so dark.

"They're also in their forties, well established in careers, and generally more settled in life. I'm... too close to your age for social services to have been entirely comfortable with me keeping you, and if you'd been even a bit younger I wouldn't have been allowed to." I took a deep breath and let it out slowly. "If they think you're not being cared for here..." I trailed off. The thought was just another added level of stress to all of this. No, Emma's caseworker hadn't said anything yet, probably never would, but they could take her away if they really wanted to and her constantly falling asleep in class wouldn't help my case if the occasion ever came up.

Emma looked stricken as she considered what I was saying. "They can't take me away because I'm not sleeping! That's not... it's not fair!"

"Life's not fair, Ems," I said. "I'm not saying that anyone's said anything yet, because they haven't, but I am saying that it's something to keep in mind."

Her eyes watered a bit and she swallowed. "Right," she said, and stared down at her plate. "I'm sorry, Jamie. I'll try harder to sleep at night."

The worst part was that I knew that she was lying. She wasn't going to sleep more because she was too busy sneaking out killing evil plant monsters. Maybe part of it was not being able to sleep because of the accident, but the majority of it was her trying to save the world. Or whatever, because I refused to think of her as a superhero, dammit.

I said nothing about the lie I knew I'd just been told, and instead smiled at her. "I know you will," I said.

The rest of dinner was quiet, and we hung out together in the living room as she did homework and we watched whatever was on the television. She went up to bed at ten o'clock and I stayed downstairs for a few hours, alternating my attention between a good book and the sitcom currently playing on the television.

Neither were enough to distract me from the sound of her swearing after dropping to the ground outside, but I didn't go after her and I tried not to dwell on it. Hopefully she'd come back and get some sleep so that she'd stop falling asleep in class.

I didn't hear her going back into her room until almost four in the morning, and even then I couldn't quite make myself sleep.

*   *   *

I had a session with Gabrielle the next day. It was rough because there was so much that I just couldn't tell her without landing myself in a facility somewhere. Tree spirits? No way. My sister having special powers? Not the best idea to talk about that. Me having special powers? Nope. Not a word of it could be said to her. So we basically talked about how little luck I was having getting Emma to sleep. She gave me some advice, including some over the counter medications that might be helpful if I couldn't convince her to come in and be evaluated, then the session was over and I headed back home.

Emma was waiting at home, because my sessions with Gabrielle always interfered with being home for Emma after school, but I had to go when she had openings. She was sitting at the kitchen table with two glasses of chocolate milk and what smelled like fresh chocolate chip cookies.

I stared at her, my eyes widening. "What did you do?" I asked as I slid into the seat across from her.

She looked offended but the expression didn't last too long and she handed me a note. "My guidance counselor wants to meet with you next week," she said with a grimace.

"You fell asleep in class again?" I hazarded as I stared at the formal looking note.

"Yeah," she said and had the grace to look ashamed. "I'm so sorry Jamie. I tried drinking some Red Bull, but it didn't really do any good. I mean it did, but just until I hit the caffeine crash, and then it was just miserable."

I closed my eyes. "This is okay," I said, though it was anything but. "You have to know that he's going to want to know what I'm doing to help you with this."

"You're helping me so much!" Emma said immediately.

"Yeah. But he's going to want you to see a therapist, and Ems, I'm not sure that I disagree with him." Even knowing what I did about her extracurricular activities, even knowing that was why she was so tired all the time, I still thought she needed to see someone. She'd been in the car, after all, and I'd heard her nightmares when she'd first come home, and when she actually slept at night.

"I'll think about it," she said, but she didn't sound convinced.

"Emma!"

She jerked her head up at my irritated exclamation. I tried not to yell at her, tried not to get frustrated, but dammit I needed her to understand how bad this could be.

"They can take you from me," I said as clearly as I could. "He can file a report with CPS. In fact, if he thinks I'm neglecting you or hurting you or anything then he's obligated to do so. So I need you to agree to see a therapist so that when I meet with him I can tell him that I've already got you seeing someone."

Emma blinked at me. "I guess," she said finally, reluctantly. "If you really think it'll help."

I did, and so I called Gabrielle's office while Emma was sitting with me and made her an appointment for Monday after school with Adriana, a perfectly nice woman that Gabrielle had mentioned when last we'd spoke about Emma needing a therapist. So today. Since my appointment with her guidance counselor was apparently next Tuesday, that worked well. I could honestly tell him that she was seeing a therapist, and hopefully nothing would come of the meeting other than my having a pretty clear view of exactly how Emma was doing in school now that Mom and Dad were gone.

The rest of the night was tense and it only got worse when I heard her sneaking out the window again. I wanted to go after her, to tell her to let it go for just one night, but I didn't. It wouldn't help, because I knew my sister. It would only make her angrier, only make her more determined to keep trying.

Instead I closed my eyes and tried to get some sleep.

*　　　*　　　*

I must have succeeded because I blinked open my eyes at one point to the sound of soft tapping on my bedroom window. Since there wasn't really a tree out there or anything the sound startled me all the way awake and I sat up and stared at the window. Leaf was sitting on the window sill, staring at me with his eerily glowing golden eyes.

"Shit," I muttered, and stood up. I crossed the room and opened the window. "What?" I asked, a bit cross.

"Still want to help Emma?" he asked.

I blinked the last of the sleep from my eyes. "Yes," I said immediately without hesitation.

"Then get dressed and meet me downstairs." Leaf jumped nimbly from the window and I stared after him for a second. Then I shut the window, got dressed, and met him downstairs as he'd asked. "Open your senses for me and tell me what you feel."

I tried to do as he asked. I normally tried pretty hard to ignore this part of me, so deliberately using it was a bit harder than I cared to admit. But I managed it and I could suddenly feel so much more than I was used to. It took my breath away and I struggled to filter the emotions. Leaf was with me, and his emotions were green and strong and soothing and I'm not even the slightest bit embarrassed to admit that I grounded myself on him.

Then I felt what I was pretty sure was what he was looking for. "I can feel something... terrible," I said. I turned in its direction. It felt like rage and hatred and something sick and rotten and disgusting. It was literally the worst thing I'd ever felt in my life.

"That's not what you're looking for," Leaf said immediately. His hand touched my shoulder and I was grounded in him again suddenly. "That's the thing your sister is dealing with tonight. But nice job sensing that."

"Thanks, I think." I tried not to imagine my sister dealing with something so angry, so hateful. Unfortunately, I'd always had a fairly vivid imagination and once I started it was almost impossible to stop. I took a deep breath. "So what am I supposed to be looking for?"

"It might be too difficult for you to separate him from that thing," Leaf said, for once not sounding condescending. "I'll just take you to him."

I didn't argue. Touching that thing with my mind was actually leaving me a bit off kilter I was pretty sure. I could feel a sort of queasiness that I wasn't familiar with, and my mind felt almost oily. It was a hard sensation to describe.

Leaf started walking and I followed. It wasn't a very long walk, and we actually did wind up in the park I'd expected to go to when tracking Emma earlier in the week. There was a tree there, or what would have been a tree. It was braced with sticks, but Leaf let out a small hiss when he saw it. "He won't make it," Leaf said quietly.

"He's dying?" I asked. I took a step forward, drawn to the tree that was sadly listing in its ties.

"His roots are already gone," Leaf said. He stepped forward with me and as we approached the tree something flickered and appeared before us. "They've killed him."

My breath caught. I'd expected someone like Leaf, not what I got. He was small and fragile and didn't look a day over five years old. He was crying, and his grief hit me like a punch to the gut. I had to make myself start breathing again and it was one of the hardest things I'd ever done.

"Hi there," I said, and approached him.

He said nothing, but kept crying. There was something stirring in his grief, a low and dark and dangerous undercurrent of anger. I could see what Leaf meant about him maybe being a problem after the fact because I recognized something in that anger akin to the thing that Emma was dealing with tonight. I could also feel his sickness. It was a creeping undertone of wrong that made me shudder.

"I'm James," I tried.

The sapling let out a wail and rushed me. He might have intended to hurt me, I don't know, but as it was I just caught him and pulled him close and let him pummel my chest with his tiny little fists. It didn't even hurt. What hurt more was the way his feelings amplified with contact, but it was okay. I was okay. I could handle this.

He stopped hitting me eventually and sagged against me, his sobs quieting into sniffling. "I'm sorry," I said honestly to him. I wasn't sure what else to say.

He let out a hiccupping little laugh. "Me too," he said. "Those kids were so mean. They pulled on me and pushed me and kicked me and now I..." He stopped, his words devolving into broken sobs once more.

"That's pretty horrible," I said quietly, and rubbed at his back. He was clinging to me now, and as his sobs petered off I realized that it wasn't because he was calming down but because he was too tired to keep going. I could feel the creeping sickness getting worse. He wasn't going to make it through the night.

I sat down and he went down with me, almost falling into my lap. I glanced over and saw Leaf standing quietly, leaning against a tree, watching me with something I couldn't name in his gaze. I turned my attention back to the sapling.

"What's your name?" I asked him.

"Don't have one," the sapling said. He let out another tiny sob and said, "Nobody ever gave me a name."

I swallowed the lump that rose in my throat. "I'm so sorry," I said again. I closed my eyes and ran my fingers through his leafy green hair and tried to think soothing thoughts. It worked, and I felt him relax against me. "I'll stay with you, if you'd like," I said. I could tell that it wasn't going to be long.

"Please," the little one said. "I don't want to be alone." He let out another tiny little sob and burrowed closer.

I focused very hard on projecting soothing, peaceful thoughts and his sobs stopped and he rested against me. "You won't be alone," I said quietly, and continued to stroke his tiny little head. "I'm here, and so is Leaf. We're going to stay with you until it's over."

The sickness was spreading now, and the sapling looked like he was dying. His hair in my hands was turning brown and his skin was fading to an ashy sort of grey. I continued to stroke him and murmur soothingly to him as I felt his light flicker, then slowly fade to nothingness. His body crumbled in my arms and I was left with nothing but the memory of him there.

I stared at where he'd been until Leaf touched my shoulder. "You did well with him," Leaf said. "He won't be a vengeful spirit."

I stared up at him and tried to shake off the despair that wanted to creep over me. I had done this to help Emma, and I was glad that I'd given the tiny sapling some peace. I'd done a good thing tonight.

So why did I feel so terrible?

Leaf helped me to my feet which was pretty good because I honestly wasn't sure if I would have stood without him there. He led me back to the house and left me once the door was shut behind me. I headed upstairs, my motions practically mechanical. I changed back into my pajamas and curled up in my bed and hoped that the clawing, snarling pit of despair in the bottom of my stomach would just go away because I had no idea what to do about it.

I had done a good thing. I had prevented more of a burden from falling on my sister, and I'd soothed a broken spirit to its eternal rest, whatever that might entail. I'd done something inarguably good tonight. So why couldn't I shake the awful feelings that were rattling around inside of me?

I pulled the pillows over my head and huddled under the covers and tried to stop shivering. I'd done something good.

I repeated that to myself over and over and over again and maybe if I kept saying it I would eventually be able to make myself believe it.

Chapter Four: Aftermath

Someone was knocking on my door.

I blinked. The room was bright. When had that happened?

"Jamie?" Emma called.

It must be time for her to go to school. I made myself get out of bed, my whole body resisting the effort. I didn't want to get up. I didn't want to move. I just wanted to go curl up in bed again. I shuffled in the general direction of the door, my feet barely leaving the floor to walk. I opened it and leaned against the frame of the door. "Hey, Ems," I said quietly.

"Jesus!" She stared at me, her eyes wide. "Maybe you should get some more sleep," she said. "You look like shit, Jamie."

I stared blankly at her. She stared back at me and I realized that she was waiting for a response. "That's... probably a good idea."

She went up on her tiptoes to feel my forehead. "Maybe you should go to the doctor," she said, her hand pressed against my skin.

"Not sick," I said, even as I fought the urge to lean into the touch. I could feel her concern, warm and soft and sweet, and I wanted to wrap myself in it. It almost helped, but then underneath there was the anger and pain and...

I wrenched away from her with a small gasp. "I should go back to bed," I told her.

"Right," she muttered. "You probably should." She was frowning now, and she reached out to touch my shoulder. "Get some more sleep, and hopefully you'll feel better when I get back."

She left, and moments later I heard the door close downstairs. I should get up. I should eat something, do something. I couldn't really find the energy to make myself do much of anything. Instead I shuffled slowly back to the bed, my bones aching with the chill of the room. Maybe I was sick. What else could explain the way I was feeling? Sickness was the only option.

I curled up under the covers again. They helped with the chill and the ache, but not much. I was tired but I couldn't make myself sleep. Every time I closed my eyes I could hear that poor little sapling crying. I could feel him dying over and over and over again and it made me want to scream so I opened my eyes and stared at nothing because that was the only thing I could do.

I heard a tapping on the window. I could see who it was without moving so I looked and it was Leaf. He was staring at me, brow furrowed in what was maybe concern, maybe something else. The glass between us muffled his emotions and I was too tired to see if I could feel what he was feeling. And too frightened to try. He noticed me looking and tapped again, a bit more fervently, and I thought that maybe I should get up and let him into the room.

I didn't move. The thought of getting out of bed was almost enough to make me physically ill. I curled up and ignored the tapping until it stopped, then felt vaguely bad about it. I had some idea that time was passing, that there were needs I had that I wasn't attending, but nothing seemed urgent enough to try getting out of bed for. I was warm, at least close to it, and leaving the bed seemed like it would bring back that terrible chill.

Eventually my eyes slipped closed and time must have passed because I heard the door open downstairs. "Jamie?" Emma called.

I couldn't find the energy to respond. I knew that I should, knew that I was just going to make her more worried about me, knew that I was going to add to her burdens, but I just couldn't make myself say anything.

I heard her come up the stairs, heard her tap on my door. I must not have closed it all the way, or maybe I hadn't really closed it at all, because it creaked open at her touch. "Jamie?" she said again, a hushed whisper.

I felt awful because I knew that I was scaring her. I just...
"Emma," I said quietly. The word was just about all that I
could manage.

"You okay?" She crossed the room. I could feel her standing
next to me, could feel the gentle concern flowing off of her in
waves. Could feel her fear, too, and a sense of urgency
beneath that. I was making everything so much worse.

"I'll be fine," I said. My voice came out as little more than a
croak. I'd neither eaten nor drank anything the entire day. I
was honestly surprised that I managed to say anything at all
given that.

"You said that before I left, and it doesn't look like you've
moved at all." She climbed up on the bed behind me and
poked my shoulder. "Seriously, Jamie, have you left the bed
since I left for school?"

I shook my head. I wanted to respond out loud, to reassure
her, but the effort of doing so seemed more than I could
handle at the moment.

"Did you eat anything today?" she asked, then she laughed.
"No, of course you haven't. Not if you haven't left the bed."
She tugged on my shoulder then. "Come on, get up, let's get
some food in you."

I sighed and let myself be manhandled to my feet. I made it
to the door once more, then I stopped. "I'm not hungry,
Ems," I tried.

She shoved me in the back, forcing me to stumble out of the room. "You haven't eaten all day. Don't give me that shit. You're going to eat something, even if it's just soup. And you're going to drink a glass of water, and maybe then you can go back to bed."

I sighed and made my way slowly down the stairs. The couch in the living room looked almost as nice as my bed, and I sat on it before Emma could get any bright ideas about making me cook. Cooking... no. That wasn't going to happen.

She stood in front of me, her hands on her hips, then she sighed. "Alright, fine," she said. "I'll make you some soup. And you'll eat it, and you'll like it even if it's not your favorite kind, okay?"

I blinked at her. "Yes," I agreed. Arguing was too much effort.

She disappeared in the kitchen, and then she was back with a glass of water in one hand and a steaming mug in the other. Had she been gone long enough to cook? I didn't think she had. But the soup in her hand certainly implied that she had. I should probably be concerned if I was losing time like that. That was definitely something I should worry about.

"Jamie!" she snapped. The soup was on the coffee table and so was the water and she was kneeling in front of me. Emma was frowning, her brow furrowed in concern. I was really, really losing it. "Jamie, do I need to call an ambulance?" she asked, her voice wavering.

I made an effort because I didn't want her to be afraid and I didn't want to make her cry. "I'm fine, Emma. Just not feeling great." I tried on a smile.

Bad idea. She paled a bit. "Okay," she whispered. "I guess let's get some food in you." She pressed the mug of soup into my hand and I tried to take a sip.

It was hot, but other than that it didn't really taste like anything. Like ashes, maybe. Ashes and bad dreams. I didn't want to eat it. Still, I did my best and managed to choke down about half of it before giving up. The glass of water was easy to finish after that.

Then I stared pleadingly at Emma. "I want to go back to bed," I said to her. It was cold. I was freezing, and I was pretty sure my teeth were about to start chattering.

Emma closed her eyes. "Okay," she said, but it was reluctant. "If you're still like this tomorrow then we're going to be spending our Saturday at the hospital, okay?"

I just blinked at her and stood up. She shadowed me as I made my way back upstairs which was probably a good thing because I almost fell once or twice. She steadied me with quick, gentle hands, and helped me back into bed once we reached it. She pulled the covers up over me and kissed my forehead.

"Do you want me to stay?" she asked, her voice soft with worry.

I stared up at her. Did I want her to stay? Of course I did. I wanted her where I could keep an eye on her. But her emotions hurt because her worry was abrasive, and she had this undercurrent of grief probably left from our parents death and anger and some other things that I couldn't identify that all hurt me more than her concern warmed me.

"Better not," I said. My voice was slow but it came out less rusty than it had earlier. The soup and the water had probably helped. I even had the energy for a proper excuse. "If I'm sick you shouldn't catch it."

She sighed and nodded. "Okay," she said. "Just... I'll stay in tonight, even if I can't sleep. Get some rest, and call me if you need anything, okay?"

"I will," I said. I probably wouldn't. I ached and just wanted to close my eyes and sleep. Maybe forever. Forever sounded really good right now, actually.

She was gone when I opened my eyes and the room was dark. Mostly dark. Like it was twilight, maybe. Had I fallen asleep? I didn't know. What had woken me up? I didn't hear any movement from the house so that couldn't be it. What-

"Hey there," Leaf said quietly to me. He was kneeling right in front of me, his shiny golden eyes glowing in the dark. "How are you feeling?"

"Fine," I said, though nothing could be further from the truth. I was tired. Exhausted still. My body ached, and I kept feeling everything. I could still feel Emma even though she wasn't in the room, her emotions whirling chaotically inside of her. How did people live like that?

"Stop!" Leaf bit out.

I jerked and focused on him and only him. He was steady and smooth and strong and even though he'd snapped at me he didn't feel angry at all. There was concern, of course there was concern, but no anger. Just warmth and kindness and concern and maybe something that felt almost like affection.

The warmth was what drew me in. I needed more of it. Desperately. I must have made a noise, said something, because Leaf groaned at me. "You foolish little human," he muttered, and then he was moving. He shoved me further back into the bed and climbed in with me. The feelings, as with Emma and with the sapling before her, amplified with his touch. But unlike with Emma there was no dark undercurrent to him. He was warm and safe and so very alive that it made me shudder against him.

He didn't say anything, but just held me for a long time. He smelled like grass and flowers and living things and felt much the same. I relaxed into his hold and closed my eyes, and eventually I woke up and the room had gone completely dark. I almost felt alive again, and winced to remember how worried Emma had been about me during the day.

"It wasn't your fault," Leaf said. He was awake and staring up at the ceiling and I was still curled up embarrassingly close to him.

"What?" I asked, a bit surprised.

"Your behavior today. It wasn't your fault. It was, in fact, mine. I had never anticipated that your empathy was as strong as it is. Most humans barely have the gift, but yours..." He trailed off.

"I don't understand," I said. Because I didn't, and Leaf probably thought I was an idiot anyway so I might as well fess up to it.

He sighed and rolled onto his side so that he was facing me. He put one arm around my waist so that he was still touching me, pulling me into an almost intimate embrace. It was... nice.

"The death of the sapling affected you more than I had imagined it would," he said patiently, his voice low and gentle. "Your depression is an aftereffect of feeling another living being die. You felt him fade to nothing, now there's a part of you that wants to fade to nothing. Being around living things helps, but your sister is too raw emotionally to do you much good. You need something steadier."

"Nothing is much steadier than an oak," I said, then flushed. It almost sounded like I was flirting with the tree spirit. That... was a terrible idea, actually. Aside from potentially offending the only person who knew his way around Emma's talent and my own, there was the fact that relationships never worked out for me. And Leaf didn't really like me anyway.

He didn't seem offended though, and instead let out a small snort of laughter. "Exactly so," he said. "You're feeling better I take it?"

"I am," I said. And I was. The cloud that had covered me for most of the day seemed like it was gone and I felt awful for the way I'd worried Emma earlier.

"Good," Leaf said. Still, he made no move to move and I didn't try to encourage him to do so. I hadn't been held like this in a very long time, not since things had fallen apart with Maya four years ago. It was nice.

Finally, I knew that I had to say something because this had the potential to get incredibly awkward. "Not that I mind having you here, but-"

"You're feeling fine now, but I'm not sure that the depression is entirely out of your system," Leaf said before I could finish. "So I'll stay the rest of the night, and that should be more than enough to stabilize you completely." He paused, then cleared his throat and sounded almost shy when he asked, "Unless you've an objection?"

"No, that's fine," I said quickly.

I drifted off to sleep in his arms, and when I woke in the morning he was gone and I was terribly embarrassed. Still, there was nothing to be done about it, so I got up and resolved to not mention this other than maybe to thank him later for helping me through the night.

I went downstairs and started breakfast, despite some lingering exhaustion from the day before. Part of me was tempted to simply lay in bed and wait for Emma to come find me again, but I didn't want to make her worry any more than I already had.

It was worth it to see the smile on her face when she thundered down the stairs twenty minutes after I started frying the pancakes.

"Feeling better?" she asked eagerly even as she started setting the table.

"So much better," I said to her, and grinned at her. "Sorry about yesterday."

She scoffed at me. "Whatever," she said. "You're allowed to have a day like that once in a while, brother mine." Then she laughed, loud and bright. "But just one. Which means you've used up your quota for at least a month, got it?"

"Got it," I said, and fell into the easy rhythm of a sleepy Saturday at home.

Chapter Five: Time Doing What it Does Best

A week passed, and I felt like a human again by the end of it. I met with Emma's guidance counselor, told him honestly that she was seeing a therapist, and that I was working on helping her sleep some more. It helped that Emma managed to stay awake in class after that meeting, mostly because she seemed to be coming in earlier at night. And I think her first meeting with Adriana really had helped, even if she had been reluctant to give it a try.

Leaf showed up at my window a week later, and I was embarrassed to see him. When I blushed and stammered at him, he glowered at me. "Stop. You were in a rough place and it was partially my fault. Don't feel bad about needing my help."

I relaxed a bit. He wasn't embarrassed, so why should I be? "Still, thanks," I said to him.

"You're welcome." Then he looked away and cleared his throat. "Let's just try not to let it happen this time, okay?"

"You need me again?" I perked up a bit. Not that I wanted another plant to be dying so I could help him or her or it find peace, but I wanted to do something. Emma thought I hadn't noticed, but she'd definitely come home with bruises the other night. I didn't want her to be hurt.

"Yeah. It shouldn't be so bad this time." Leaf fidgeted, then added, "But if it is, you need to tell me before I leave you. I'm an oak. I can handle the influx of your emotions and ground you. Letting yourself fall that deeply into despair is a dangerous thing."

"Why?" I hadn't really been that despairing, I didn't think. I'd mostly been tired. Which had been a pain, of course it was, but it wasn't the worst thing to ever happen to me.

And now Leaf was looking at me like I was an idiot. "Because, you idiot, people kill themselves when they're feeling like that."

I blinked at him. "I was just tired. I wasn't thinking of killing myself," I said, honestly confused.

"And if that feeling had continued for weeks? Months? Might you have been tempted to look for a way to end it all then?"

Shudders wracked my body at the thought. "Emma would have done something before-"

"Emma can't help you with your empathy," Leaf said severely. "I can. Which is why you tell me when you feel your emotions getting that out of control again. If you don't think you can handle that, then we're done. I won't be responsible for your death."

"Understood," I said. I didn't want to stop. I wanted to help Emma, and yes, maybe help some sad little saplings too.

"Good." Leaf took a deep breath and let it out. "Now. As I was saying, I have someone for you to come visit. An angry spirit this time. A friend of the sapling, actually, from last week. He's grieving, but that grief has lately started to turn violent. If you can calm him, he might not require a visit from your sister."

Right. Grieving spirit. Because it's not like I had any experience dealing with grief personally or anything like that. I could definitely handle this. "Okay, awesome. Let's go."

I followed Leaf back to the park, and again he stood off to one side as I spoke to the grieving, infuriated spirit. He was much bigger than the sapling had been, easily towering over both Leaf and I. And he was angry, so very angry. His entire body vibrated with it, and there was a dull thrum of anger in the back of my mind constantly during the conversation.

"They're murderers!" He roared at me, his voice hurting my ears. "Even if your pathetic human justice doesn't acknowledge them as such, that's exactly what they are! They killed him before he even had a chance to live, and you're asking me to just let them go?"

51

"I'm not denying that they did something awful," I said, holding my hands up in the universal gesture for peace. "I'm just saying that they're young and stupid, and they'll never have the chance to learn if you just kill them."

He let out an inarticulate shout of rage. "My friend will never have a chance to learn because of them! He'll never have a chance to grow! Why do they deserve-"

"Because they didn't know any better!" I shouted, then winced. Shouting at something that looked like it could bench press me didn't seem like the wisest of ideas. But it worked. The spirit was staring at me like he'd never seen me before. I seized my advantage. "I'm not saying that what they did was right, because of course it wasn't. But they didn't know there was something alive inside of that tree. Something sentient, I mean. They're not monsters. They wouldn't just kill someone if they'd known that was what they were doing."

"He screamed," the spirit said, but his voice was small. "He screamed and screamed and begged and they wouldn't stop. How can you say they didn't know?" He was shrinking, though, much as the spirit my sister had dealt with on that first night had shrunk. And his anger was giving way to confusion, judging by his feelings.

"Humans can't see you guys," I said carefully. "I didn't even know you existed until I followed my sister one night and Leaf approached me, and I'm apparently actually able to see you. If they'd known, they wouldn't have hurt the sapling."

He shrank even further, until I was looking at a being who could have been my age, or Leaf's age, and looked very similar. The anger was entirely gone from him, leaving a manageable, healthy level of grief and a sort of frustration that I could understand because I dealt with it all the time when dealing with Emma.

"You should tell them," he said. His words were slower now, more thoughtful. Leaf, I noticed, had relaxed entirely and was no longer paying attention to the conversation and was instead examining a patch of flowers, something like a smile on his face. I guess that meant I was out of danger.

"They'd lock me away," I told the spirit. "Humans have pretty clear ideas about insanity, and they'd all think me mad."

"Humans are frustrating," the tree spirit said.

"Preach," I said glumly. Hell, I was a human and I barely understood us most of the time. I couldn't imagine how alien we were to plant spirits.

"We should go," Leaf said suddenly. He was by my side again and I hadn't even realized. "Jamie is tired," he added in explanation to the spirit.

The spirit seemed saddened at the statement, for reasons that I'd probably never understand. "I thank you for your explanation," he said to me. "I'm glad that I didn't hurt anyone in my rage."

"I'm glad that I was able to help," I told him, and smiled. Now that Leaf had pointed it out, I did suddenly feel exhausted. It wasn't like the last time, though. This was a genuine sort of exhaustion, not that strange fog that had settled over me.

"Stop by and see me sometime," the spirit suggested. "My tree provides nice shelter on sunny days."

I smiled. "I'll do that," I told him. He bowed to me, then, and faded back into one of the larger trees in the park. "Do all the trees have spirits?" I asked Leaf as we started walking.

"Most," Leaf said, glancing around them. He paused and rested one hand against a tree on the way back to the house. "Some of them have lost their spirits. Sometimes they go wandering and forget to come back or lose their way. This tree's spirit has been gone for almost fifty years. She went on a journey and hasn't yet returned. If she stays away too long, her tree will die and so will she."

"That's sad." I stared at the tree. It seemed perfectly healthy. "How long does she have?"

Leaf shrugged and started walking again. "It varies."

That was all he would say on the matter, and when we arrived at the house he looked at me closely. "You don't need me to stay," he said, sounding certain.

"I think I'm okay," I agreed. "Just tired, as you so helpfully pointed out."

"Good. Let me know if you feel yourself falling into that fog again, but I think you'll be okay." Leaf walked away from me, and I felt curiously disappointed as I watched him fade back into his tree.

I shook off the feeling and headed into the house to get some rest. I'd done a good deed and I'd earned it.

*   *   *

Time, as it tends to do, passed. I stopped getting reports from the school about Emma, and it wasn't just because winter break was approaching and the teachers no longer had the energy to care what the hooligans they taught did with their time. Leaf sent me out to deal with a few more minor problems, and I was getting fairly good at it. None of them managed to hurt me the way that first one had, which meant that Leaf hadn't spent a night in my bed since. And that was a good thing.

Really, that was a great thing.

Anyway, about a month after I figured out what my sister was up to late at night, I realized that life was actually sort of coming together. Emma was doing okay. I was doing okay.

"And isn't that supposed to be a good thing?" Leaf asked me, leaning against his tree trunk, his feet up on the branch and almost halfway in my lap. His hair had turned a most glorious array of colors, from reds to golds to almost purples.

It was amazing, and I half wondered if he'd go bald when winter hit fully. I didn't dare ask him.

"It's a great thing," I said, kicking my feet and trying to ignore the five foot drop below me. It hadn't seemed like such a long drop when I'd been a teenager. "I just don't know what to do next."

Leaf sighed. "And for some reason figuring this out requires you to sit in my tree?" He sounded annoyed, but when I glanced at him I could see a small smile on his face. When I focused, I could feel the warmth of his amusement and that almost-affection feeling.

"Is that a problem?" I asked, ignoring what I could sense from Leaf. "Because you know I used to sit in this tree all the time when I was growing up."

Leaf laughed at me, his shoulders shaking with the force of it. "You say that like I don't remember. Like I didn't watch you do it. You were adorable back then."

I blushed. "That's not really something adults like to hear," I told him.

"Pretty sure adults don't sit in trees getting career advice from plants." Leaf smirked at me. "So I guess you're not a proper adult, are you?"

"Maybe they would if they knew that plants had spirits inside of them," I said, but it was a weak counter. "Maybe I'll open a vegetarian restaurant and serve acorns."

Leaf kicked me, the blow hard enough that it might have left a bruise. "That's a horrible thing to joke about, cooking my offspring." He sniffed at me. "So few of them survive to grow into trees anyway."

"I wouldn't do that," I reassured him, patting his foot. "I'm not a good enough cook." Then I brightened, remembering a question that I'd considered as I'd been fixing dinner the other night. "What do you eat, anyway?"

Leaf stared at me, his expression telling me that I couldn't possibly be so stupid. "I'm a spirit. I don't eat."

I sagged. "Of course you don't." I'd had the half-thought to cook him a nice dinner to thank him for helping me to help Emma. Apparently that was a bust.

"I drink water though," he said. I looked at him, and he was looking away from me. His cheeks were slightly darker shade of brown than normal, and I realized he was blushing. "Different types of water taste different. Some are nicer than others."

"What's your favorite?" I asked.

He hummed as he considered. "Emma gave me one with a blue label that was particularly nice. There were some added things, but not enough to make it not be water anymore."

Blue label? That was all of them. Whatever. I'd figure it out. "Okay, cool," I said to him.

He snorted at me. "Cool?" he asked, his tone lilting and mocking.

"Cool," I said, refusing to back down from my word choice.

Leaf rolled his eyes. "Have you considered opening a greenhouse?" he asked suddenly.

I frowned at the apparent change of subject. "Huh?"

"You were saying you didn't know what to do with yourself. You could open a greenhouse. You'd be good at raising plants."

I laughed at him, I couldn't help it. Then I realized he wasn't smiling or laughing. "You're serious?" I asked.

"Of course I am," he said, with all the dignity of one who'd just been insulted. "It would be good for you to be around plants who aren't angry all the time. Or grieving, or dying."

"I'm around you," I said.

He smiled at me, the expression softer and more genuine than his other ones. "You are, aren't you?" he asked. Then his eyes widened and he started to melt back into the tree. I wanted to ask him why, but before I could he was gone.

Then Emma was opening her window. "The heck are you doing in my tree, Jamie?" she asked, staring at me with the most incredulous expression on her face I'd ever seen.

"Can't a guy hang out in a tree?" I asked, kicking my feet innocently.

Her dubious expression said it all. "Technically, sure," she said. Then she shoved at me. "Scoot over, I'll come out with you."

I shifted over until I was sitting where Leaf had been only moments before. The space felt oddly warm. It was nice. "How was your day?" I asked her.

She hopped out onto the branch without a care for her own safety and plopped down next to me. "Good," she said. "I think I might get an after school job now that I'm sleeping more often. What do you think?"

I considered the matter. "I'd rather you didn't," I said honestly. "It's not like we need the money." We didn't. We'd... well, I hated to think of it like this, but the accident had left us with more money than we could ever use no matter what we did with it. The woman who'd hit mom and dad had paid... a lot more than they would have ever earned in their lifetimes.

"Yeah, but I want to do something after school, and none of the clubs really interest me. Not to mention I couldn't really try out for them while I was still restricted from some activities." She'd been cleared two weeks after school started for most things, but by then it had been too late for the fall sports. I glanced over at her. She was now kicking her feet as I'd done and looked like she was considering jumping out of the tree.

She probably would, too. "I was thinking of opening a greenhouse," I said hastily. While I hadn't meant to say that, it wasn't the worst idea in the world. I'd always loved plants, after all. "Maybe you could help me with that once I get it started."

She smiled at me. "I'd like that."

I felt a warm glow of approval coming from the tree and I realized that even though we couldn't see him, Leaf was there listening to the conversation. That approval, while I didn't need it, felt amazing and made my heartbeat tick up just a little bit. There was the smallest chance that I was in more trouble with Leaf than I'd realized, and I should probably do something about that.

What exactly I should do was a concern for another time, though, as I got to watch Emma jump out of the tree. I knew she was going to do that, but it didn't make my heart rate go down at all, only back up. "Seriously?" I called down to her.

She laughed up at me. "Come on, Jamie, you can do it! Just jump down. I know you did it when you were my age!"

"That was a long time ago!" I protested. But I swung my legs around and wondered if I could still manage the jump without hurting myself. It really wasn't that far, after all.

"Come on, or are you a coward?" she asked.

Well. I couldn't let that stand, could I? I jumped. The skinned knee I got was almost worth it to watch her laugh with surprise when I actually did it.

Chapter Six: My Sister is not a Superhero!

It couldn't last, of course. Things were going too well.

It was three in the morning when I got the call, and I'd actually been sleeping for once. In fact, it didn't even register for me immediately that there was a phone call. I thought I was dreaming, and it was only when the ringing immediately started once more that I made myself open my eyes. My cell was going, and when I picked it up and stared at it through bleary eyes I realized that I didn't know the number.

It was probably a wrong number. I dropped the cell to the bed and covered my eyes with my hand and hoped that whoever had called me twice realized that I wasn't going to pick up.

And then it rang a third time, and I sighed. Apparently somebody couldn't take a hint.

"Hello?" I asked.

"Is this James Gardner?" The voice was male and authoritative and I frowned.

"Who's calling?" I asked instead of answering. My heartbeat picked up. This was sounding frighteningly like... no. No, it couldn't be. Emma was fine, I was just imagining things. Making parallels where none existed. It was a trick of my sleepy mind.

"This is Doctor Johnson from Cedar Point. James, listen, I'm calling because your sister's been in some kind of incident-"

"Jesus Christ is she okay?" My words tumbled over each other in their speed and I jumped from the bed even as I asked the question. I had to get dressed. I needed keys. I needed to get to her. God, what if she was hurt?

"She's unconscious-"

"Is she in a coma?" My heart stopped and I froze. What if she was? Oh god, what if she was in another coma? I swallowed hard to try to put my heart back where it belonged rather than in my throat.

"It's too soon by far to start throwing around words like coma, James. If you could just come down to the hospital, then we could talk in person." Johnson had been her doctor before, and he sounded like the same one. He was good. He would tell me if it was serious.

I took a deep breath, then another. "I can be there in twenty minutes." It wasn't a long drive from the house, and at this time there would be no traffic. It wasn't like I didn't have the route memorized or anything. It got hairy around six in the morning and four in the afternoon, but at three in the morning it would be empty.

"She's currently in the ER, but we're going to admit her. Stop by the visitor's sign in, which is-"

"I know where it is," I said flatly. It wasn't like my parents hadn't spent days in the ICU there, each of them, before they'd gone. It wasn't like Emma hadn't spent a week in the ICU with them before they'd decided that she wasn't going to regain consciousness anytime soon. If there was one thing I knew, it was where the visitor's sign in was.

What the hell was I going to do if she was in a coma again?

"Then we'll see you shortly, James. Drive carefully."

"Thanks," I said, and hung up. I took several deep breaths, stripped out of my pajamas and did my best to make myself presentable. I splashed some cold water on my face, grabbed a soda for the caffeine content from the fridge, and headed for my jeep.

On the way out I stopped and stared at Leaf's tree. "You there?" I asked him. If he was he'd probably answer no matter what time it was. I didn't get the image that he slept like Emma and I did.

He didn't answer, and I honestly wasn't sure how I felt about that. I pushed him from my mind and got in the car. I took another deep breath before turning the key. The last thing I needed to do was hurt somebody because I was distracted and caused an accident. Emma needed me, now more than ever.

I started driving. The drive to Cedar Point was so familiar to me that I made it by habit. Out of town, onto the highway, three exits away and then a left after the first light. It took me fifteen minutes, and then another three to park closest to the entrance near the sign in desk. Like I said, I knew my way around the place. I just really hoped that Emma wasn't...

She wasn't. I had to stay positive, dammit.

"James." The voice startled me and I jerked my hand away from the door. Leaf. He was leaning against the wall off to one side of the deserted entrance, his arms crossed defensively.

I stepped away from the door. "You were with her," I said, the words sounding distant to me. I could feel something other than his customary unflappable calm. Guilt. Sorrow. His calm was gone. "You were with her," I repeated, staring at him.

He swallowed. "I was," he said. He wouldn't meet my gaze. His gaze was planted firmly on the flower bed between us. "She was..." He stopped and closed his eyes. "It was too strong for her."

It was too strong for her. "You were there," I said, emphasizing every word. He'd been there with her, and it was too strong for her. He'd watched my sister get hurt. He'd watched, and done what? Nothing? Why didn't he look hurt? She was just a child. He-

"You need to calm down," Leaf said, his eyes snapping up to meet mine. He stood and touched my arm.

I jerked away. "Don't you tell me what I need to do," I snapped. "You were there with my little sister when she got hurt, and here you stand like, what, like you feel sorry for her? This is your fault!"

His golden eyes widened. "My... my fault?" His voice was barely a whisper. "You think this is my fault?"

"Why wouldn't I?" I laughed at him, the noise tearing from me the force of a gunshot. "It's your guilt that I'm picking up on."

I knew I shouldn't have said it, even though I didn't really regret the words. I was too angry to regret them. He'd done this. He'd gotten my sister involved in this shit. I knew that he had, because she never would have known without his involvement.

I felt his anger flare, dark and dangerous, and he took one slow step forward. "How dare you blame me for your sister's stupidity?" he asked, his voice coming out as a low growl. He stared at me with more contempt than he'd ever had when we'd first met. "She's the one who didn't listen to me when I told her she wasn't ready to deal with it. She's the fool who rushed ahead against all of my warnings, and she's the one who nearly got herself killed being so arrogant!" He lifted his chin and looked down his nose at me. "She's the one who acted like a typical, useless piece of human shit!"

My vision went white with the force of his anger and my own and I hauled off and punched him. "Fuck you!" I snarled, and lunged forward. "She never would have started this shit if it weren't for you!"

"You're right!" he shouted, and shoved me away from him hard enough that I landed on my ass after tipping over the flowerbed. "Your sister would have started seeing the spirits eventually and would have thought she was going mad. She'd have landed in an asylum, or whatever you call them these days."

"At least she'd have been safe!" I shouted. "Not sitting in the hospital for the second time in a year, damn you!"

He laughed at me, and the sound tore through me. "That's the life you'd rather for your sister? Locked down, stuck on an endless cocktail of drugs and in a constant loop of therapy, knowing that she was mad and knowing that it would never end?" He bowed to me, a flamboyantly mocking gesture.

"In that case, you have my sincerest apologies. I never would have interfered if I'd known that was the life she wanted."

The words broke over me, an arctic wave that took my breath away. "Leaf, I-" But he was gone, leaving me sitting on the pavement alone.

I closed my eyes against the tears that wanted to fall. This wasn't the time. I had to get up, dust myself off, and go check on Emma. I could deal with Leaf later, whatever that would entail. Whether it was groveling or chopping down his tree I was legitimately unsure.

I stood and brushed the dirt off of me, then headed into the hospital. The receptionist, Alice, recognized me, for fuck's sake, and the sympathy in her eyes was almost as painful as hearing that Emma had been hurt again.

"Back again I hear," she said, her smile soft around the edges.

"Yeah, well, I guess Emma really missed the accommodations here. I don't cook the food right or something." I tried on a smile and my face didn't break, so I left it on. It would do me some good to smile as long as I could, because I might not have reason to smile once I met with Dr. Johnson.

"She's been admitted. They've got her in room 210," Alice said. "Gonna stay the night with her?"

"Probably," I said, and scrubbed at my eyes. The smile felt brittle so I let it fall away.

"I can send the nurses in with an extra blanket or two, and maybe a pillow for the chair?"

I shook my head. "Thanks, Alice, but I don't think I'm going to be able to sleep tonight." Not with the way I was feeling.

She nodded. "Go on back then," she said, and handed me my name tag.

I headed up to her room. It wasn't exactly hard to find. Dr. Johnson was waiting for me at the door to the room.

He was a short man, small and wiry with a pinched face and a brusque manner. That was fine. I didn't need to be coddled. "How is she?" I asked immediately.

He sighed. "She's most likely going to be fine," he said. "She was awake ten minutes ago, seemed to be relatively oriented. She's sleeping again, but I think that we can safely rule out the risk of a coma. She doesn't even appear to have a concussion, despite all the battering to her face."

I closed my eyes in relief. "She's going to be okay," I repeated, my voice almost embarrassingly shaky.

"She should be," Dr. Johnson confirmed with a nod. "I'd imagine you're staying the night with her?"

"Of course," I said. It hadn't been that long since he'd worked with her, and I'd been a near-constant presence at Emma's side. He probably remembered how difficult it had been to get me out of her room back then.

"I'm not surprised," he said, his voice dry. "There's an extra bed in there, James. I'd appreciate it if you used it, especially if you're staying more than one night at a time. The last thing we need is for you to collapse and scare the nurses a second time."

I laughed, the sound weak and watery. "I'll try not to scare them again," I promised.

He patted me on the shoulder as he started to walk away. "She should be fine, James," he said, and then he was gone leaving me standing in front of the door to my sister's hospital room.

It was harder than almost anything I'd ever done to walk through that door. The only thing I could remember ever being more difficult was telling her that our parents were dead, that she'd missed their funeral and her entire sophomore year of high school.

What if they were wrong? What if she wasn't going to be okay like Dr. Johnson thought? What if I went through that door and she flat lined, or she just wasn't breathing, or... I stopped the thoughts with a practiced, vicious cut. This thinking wouldn't help anyone, much less Emma.

I opened the door.

She looked so fragile on the bed, surrounded by all sorts of wires. She was breathing on her own, but was still hooked up to oxygen. There was a heart monitor beeping steadily that went with the rise and fall of her chest. She had a few IVs going, one of them dripping something that looked suspiciously like blood. Probably was blood.

Her face, as Dr. Johnson had implied, was severely battered. Her left eye looked like it was going to swell shut and the right side of her face looked like it had been scraped along the asphalt and there was a line of stitching on her forehead above the swollen eye. She had a bandage wrapped around her left forearm, and her right forearm had a massive bruise. The rest of her was covered by the hospital gown, but I doubted that all of her injuries were visible.

It was worse than I'd imagined, almost worse than how she'd looked immediately after the crash.

I dropped into the chair by her bedside and took her limp hand in my own. It didn't so much as twitch. She likely had no idea that I was there. She was unconscious, or asleep.

I realized that my vision was going blurry and I tried to blink back the tears that wanted to fall. It didn't work and I choked back a sob. Crying wasn't going to do any good. I couldn't let myself cry like this. She needed me to be strong for her, because it looked like she'd be in here for at least a few days. Emma would hate that. She hated the hospital, and I didn't blame her.

A nurse came in with a blanket for me and her sympathetic smile almost broke me. I managed to hold it together, to exchange pleasantries with her, until she finished taking Emma's vitals and left. Then I couldn't be strong anymore.

Emma was asleep.

She didn't care if I cried, so I let myself go.

I cried until I couldn't cry anymore, my head bowed over her hand, my fingers clutching at her unmoving ones. She stayed asleep the whole time, and eventually I drifted off as well, my head resting on her bed, my hand still tangled with hers, soothed to sleep by the steady, reassuring beat that told me that in spite of all of this, in spite of her unconsciousness, she was still alive.

Everything could get better as long as she was still alive.

Chapter Seven: Breaking Point

I woke to the feeling of something thumping against my head and realized that it was Emma's hand, clumsy, trying to stroke my hair.

I sat up and winced at the way my body creaked in protest. I really wasn't meant to stay folded over in these chairs anymore. It had been hard enough two years ago, but now it was just torture. "Hey," I said tiredly.

She grinned at me, the expression a bit misshapen by her swollen face. "Hey," she said, her words a bit slurred. "I'm pretty sure they have me on some really nice painkillers because I'm not feeling any of this."

I laughed, the sound a bit watery. "Yeah, probably. You're pretty beat up, Ems. Wanna talk about it?" I knew she didn't, but I had to ask.

She shook her head. "It was an accident. I'm fine." Her smile never wavered through the lie.

"What kind of accident gives you a black eye like that?" I couldn't quite manage to keep the anger out of my voice with my question, and then I felt a flare of guilt when she flinched. "Ems, I mean-"

"No, you're right," she said. She stared down at her hands. Then she sniffled a bit. "I just don't want to talk about it, okay Jamie? I don't want you to worry about me, either."

I gritted my teeth because I could feel what she was feeling, dammit, and what she was feeling was fear or sorrow or anything like that. She was totally calm. I was being manipulated, and it made my anger soar. I choked it down because there was literally nothing I could do. "I'm your big brother," I said, my voice shaking a bit with the force of my frustration. "It's my job to worry."

She felt a flash of something like triumph and I realized she was reading my anger as acquiescence. That was fine. She could think what she liked. I was done with this game. Something had to change, but I had no idea of how to make that happen.

She laughed at me, the sound bright and happy. "You should go home and get some rest," she said to me. "I'm probably going to be stuck in here for the next few days. I don't want you wasting away in here without me."

"I'm not leaving until Dr. Johnson comes and checks you out," I said immediately. In spite of my frustration with her, in spite of the fact that I wished she would just tell me what was going on and stop trying to deceive me, I wasn't willing to leave without being one hundred percent sure that she was okay.

She groaned. "Fine, whatever, you loser." She rolled her eyes.

"Don't roll your eyes with that tone of sass," I said, making her laugh a little. This time the sound was genuine and I couldn't help but smile at her. She was my sister, they were supposed to be frustrating, right?

Emma wrinkled her nose at me and opened her mouth to say something, but cut off when the door opened after a knock. The nurse came through and took her vitals, then told us that Dr. Johnson would be with us momentarily. We sat in silence until he showed up, looking far too cheerful for someone who'd been there when I came in at three in the morning.

"Did you even go home?" I asked him.

Dr. Johnson blinked at me. "No, of course not. It's only eight o'clock. I'm on duty for another three hours." Then he turned to Emma. "So, Emma, can you tell me what you remember?"

Emma blinked at him, her eyes wide. "No?" she said, the words coming out like a question.

"There are some officers who'd like to get your statement, considering that the injuries you have are consistent with an assault. Are you feeling up to talking with them?"

Emma stared at him, her mouth gaping open. "Are you serious?" she squeaked.

Dr. Johnson stared back at her, his eyebrows going up. "Is there any reason you don't want to speak with the police?"

"What?" Emma glanced wildly at me and I could have killed her because I could feel the suspicion forming in Dr. Johnson. "N-no, I just… I just don't remember what happened, that's all." She swallowed hard.

She was lying, and everyone in the room knew it. And I knew what was going to happen as a result. "Emma, you don't have anything to be ashamed of. If someone hurt you-"

"No one hurt me!" She sounded panicked, the hysteria in her voice rising. "Nobody hurt me, I just fell while I was walking last night, that's all!"

"Okay," Dr. Johnson said, the word long and slow. "If you don't remember, that's fine I suppose, but the police will still want to speak with you. Are you feeling up to that?"

"I guess?" Emma stared at me, confusion clear in her face. "I mean, I can do that, but I can't really tell them anything."

"I should let her speak with them," I said. I didn't really know what else to say.

"Actually, I think we'd like to speak with you as well," came an unfamiliar voice from the door.

I could have cried. The officers were standing in the door, one of them, a girl with short brown hair, staring at me with genuine hate in her eyes. The other looked much calmer, his look almost clinical as he stared at me. "Whatever you need," I told them, because protesting wouldn't do any good. I hadn't hit her, I'd never hurt her, and hopefully they would believe me.

The man cleared his throat. "I'm going to interview you, James, while my partner here interviews your sister. Is that okay?"

Protesting would only make me look guiltier. "As long as Emma's okay with it," I told him.

"It's fine," Emma said, her voice shaky. "But I don't know what help I can be. I don't remember much, and I'm pretty sure I just fell."

"Your injuries aren't consistent with that," the woman said. "So we'd like to ask you a few questions."

Her partner led me out of the room, and I wound up sitting across from him in an office that the hospital apparently had for visits such as this one. I'd first met my sister's caseworker in an office like this.

He cleared his throat. "I'm Officer Thomas. I'd like to ask you a few questions about what's been going on with Emma." Despite his neutral expression, I could feel his dislike of me bleeding through me. His disgust with me. He thought I'd hurt her.

I nodded, still not looking up. "Shoot," I said, and raised the cup of coffee to my lips to take a sip. It was awful. Sort of like this situation, actually.

"Your sister's injuries are pretty consistent with being beaten up," the officer said, his voice only just neutral. I chanced a glance up and he was maintaining his neutral expression, but it looked strained.

"Yeah," I said. "She's been sneaking out at night a lot. I... I keep telling her to stay in, but aside from putting bars on the windows there's not really much I can do. And I've thought about that, but she's going through a rough spot. Our parents died last year and she spent a few months in a coma."

"Can you think of anyone who might want to hurt your sister?" Officer Thomas asked. "Anyone who might have any reason at all to attack her in a dark alley?"

I shrugged. "I don't know what she was doing out there. We don't live anywhere near there, and she's been very secretive about whatever it is she's been doing when she sneaks out at night. I've worried that she was getting involved in something illegal, but I haven't found any kind of proof." Not that I'd looked. I'd always known Emma well enough to know that she wasn't on drugs or anything.

Officer Thomas smiled, his face softening. "She's a teenage girl. They do get into all kinds of trouble, don't they?" Then he sobered. "And she's probably a lot for you to handle. Your parents just died, you've taken on a huge responsibility. There's no shame if you maybe got a bit overwhelmed. If you lost your temper with her-"

"I never touched her!" The words burst from me before I could stop them. "Jesus, officer, I wouldn't! She's all I've got in this world. I've given up everything to try and take care of her." I shook my head and scrubbed at my eyes and really hoped that I didn't break down in front of him.

"I'm just saying that if you did," Officer Thomas started.

"And I'm telling you that I didn't." My words caught on the lump forming in my throat and I had to take a sip of coffee to get the words out. "I wish I knew who did. I really, really did. Maybe I should have kept trying to follow her. Maybe I should lock her window, or cut down the tree, or something."

I could feel the officer's disgust turning to sympathy, and that was something at least. "It's understandable that you're struggling with her," he said. "I'm sure things have been rough on you, dealing with a surprise teenager."

"Well, she's always been my little sister, so it's not like I didn't know how much of a brat she could be," I said, and managed a watery smile. "I didn't hurt her," I said.

"Okay," the officer said. He patted my hand. "My partner and I are probably going to be a bit longer, so why don't you go home, get a shower and get some rest, then come back later in the afternoon?"

"Can I say goodbye to her?" I asked, then flushed. My voice came out smaller than I'd intended it to.

"Of course," he said.

Saying goodbye to Emma was rough. The officer in her room still radiated hatred in my general direction, and Emma looked and felt a bit panicked when I told her that I was leaving. Still, she hugged me, told me she was fine, and sent me on my way. I didn't feel any kind of concern from her and wondered what she'd told the officer she was speaking with. She was one of the most clever people I knew. She probably wouldn't tell them anything that would get me in trouble.

The drive home was something of a blur, and I found myself pulling up in front of the house with very little memory of how I'd gotten there. I sat in the car in silence for several minutes, then made myself get out of the car. I had to shower and get some rest, then I could go check on her.

I headed into the house, but on my way in I caught sight of the tree. Leaf's tree. Leaf was probably in that tree. He probably had no idea of what I'd gone through in the past few hours. Did he even care? This was all his fault.

It was all his fault!

I let out a low, angry noise, and stalked over to the tree. Its bark was rough beneath my hands, and before I could think better of it I punched the tree. I wanted to scream, but someone would probably hear me so I hit the tree again, and then once more, and then again, until I was pummeling the tree with both fists, not even able to see from the tears that were pouring from eyes. I hit the tree until I couldn't move my arms anymore, until my hands were bloody and I couldn't stop crying.

And through it all Leaf wasn't there

I slumped to the ground and cried. This wasn't his fault. It was mine. I wasn't a good enough guardian for Emma. They probably should take her from me, because I was worthless. I couldn't even stop crying so that I could get back to her and make sure that everything really was okay.

What kind of brother was I?

Chapter Eight: Aftermath, Redux

I realized that I wasn't alone anymore until I felt a gentle hand land on my shoulder. Leaf was out of his tree, staring at me with a sympathetic expression.

I opened my mouth to say something but found that I couldn't force any words from my throat. All that emerged was a sob that I tried to choke off. Leaf stared down at me for a long, silent minute, then dropped to the ground beside me and pulled me into his arms.

I didn't fight. His arms were strong and warm and safe around me and I didn't feel the slightest hint of embarrassment about crying on his shoulder. We sat out there for what felt like forever, even after I'd run out of tears to cry. He held me until I started to draw away, and even then he seemed reluctant to release me.

"Sorry," I said to him, my voice shaking.

"Don't be." He cleared his throat. "You were upset. I don't blame you for anything that you said, even if I wish you hadn't lost your temper with me."

I laughed, a sound with no joy to it. "I wish I hadn't lost my temper with you either. It was just... the thought of Emma, in that bed again after just getting out of it... nobody should be so familiar with the hospital that the nurses still remember her name."

"No," Leaf agreed. He leaned back against his tree and stretched his legs out. I shifted so that my side was pressed against his, my back against the rough bark of the tree. "You humans, though..." He sighed.

"Us humans, what?" I glanced at him. He was staring off into the distance, his golden eyes someplace far away. I looked down at my hands, twining in my lap, and tried not to stare at him.

"You're so fragile. So very breakable. It... is worrisome, for a being such as myself." Leaf was still staring someplace far away, remembering someone or something or just having a thought that I couldn't identify.

"What do you mean?" I asked, my voice hushed. Speaking louder seemed somehow improper.

He looked at me, his eyes focusing on me with the piercing force of a laser. "Humans live for, at most, ninety or so years. I've lived for six of your generations, and I'll live for six more after you're gone, if not longer. If you or Emma have children, I'll be there to teach them about Gardening if they inherit the gift. I'll be there to teach your children's children, and their children after that. And you'll be dead and gone."

I leaned more heavily against the tree and shifted so that I was closer to Leaf. "That must be hard for you," I said. I wanted to wrap an arm around his shoulders, then wondered why I was hesitating. I did so, and Leaf burrowed against me the moment I did so.

"You humans…" He sighed again, and I felt a tremor run through his body. "Your father was my best friend when he was a child, you know?"

I hadn't known that, actually. My father had never, never mentioned the spirit who lived in our tree. I was pretty sure I'd remember if he had.

"We laughed and played together. It was horribly undignified of me, of course, considering that at that point I was more than five hundred years old, but I didn't mind. He was such a happy child, full of life and love. And then he grew up. And, as children tend to do, he forgot about me. I was just his childhood imaginary friend, after all." Leaf fell silent. "That's probably why he never told you about me. He probably didn't remember."

My heart ached for him. "I'm sorry," I said, not sure of what else to say.

Leaf shrugged. "It's not your fault," he said. "It's just how humans are. Especially when they don't have the gift to see us as they age, like you and your sister do."

82

We sat there in silence, my arm around his shoulders and his head resting against my shoulder. I let my eyes fall closed and relaxed against the tree and against Leaf.

Finally, Leaf said, "I want you to know that it was one of the hardest decisions I ever made, telling your sister about her powers."

"Huh?" I opened my eyes to stare at him again.

He was staring off into the distance once more, a frown tugging at his lips. "Your sister had already been through so much. Just because neither one of you saw me didn't mean that I didn't see you, after all. I watched you while she was in her coma, struggling through the funeral and the lawyers and everything. And I watched her after she came home, watched her re-learn how to walk and how to run and never learn how to be a child again because that year was stolen from her. Gardeners, particularly in an area like this one where there are so many angry spirits, don't tend to live long and easy lives. They live rough and die young, and I thought that Emma had come close enough to doing that without my telling her about her powers. The last thing I wanted was to add to her burdens, and to yours."

"Why did you?" My words, this time, weren't accusatory. I wanted to know why he'd told her, but I didn't blame him for doing so. Not now that I was rational. Well. As rational as I ever was.

He curled in on himself, staring down at his hands in his lap. "Because things were getting worse. You must've noticed the rising crime rate, especially the unsolved ones. Police can't catch angry spirits. Emma could do something about it, and I thought that she might want to. Especially since the crash, the coma, definitely had an effect on her abilities. I haven't seen a Gardener like her before. She's strong, James."

"Not strong enough to fight off that thing last night," I said before I could stop myself, the words just flowing out of me.

Leaf didn't take it badly. He laughed, the sound soft and gentle, like leaves rustling in the wind. "No, not strong enough for that. She won't be ready to take on a spirit like that for a very long time." He took a deep breath. "I'm sorry that my telling her put your sister in danger."

"I know that you didn't tell her to put her in danger," I said, because I thought that it needed saying. "You're right. Crime was going up, and I'd be lying if I said that I didn't notice it going back down. Less unsolved assaults and homicides. Our sleepy town is back to being sleepy again, and if that's because of Emma then... well, I don't think I'll ever be happy that she's doing what she's doing, but I can learn to live with it."

"Good." Leaf shifted against me, then pulled away. He seemed reluctant to do so, given by speed at which he moved which was, to say the least, incredibly slow.

I took a deep breath and let it out, then took another. "I can't let it keep going like this, though."

Leaf tensed, I could see it in the line of his spine. "What do you mean?" He didn't turn back to look at me.

"She's my little sister, Leaf. I'm supposed to take care of her, and I can't do that if she's going out into danger and I'm lying in bed waiting for her to get back." I looked down at my hands. I was knotting them together and I hadn't even realized it. I made an effort to pull them apart, then glanced back up at Leaf.

He'd turned and was staring at me. "You are helping," Leaf said. "You deal with problems before they become problems. That's helping her so much, even if she doesn't know about it."

"And I'm not saying that I don't want to continue doing that," I said, my words tumbling over themselves in an effort to leave my lips. "I'm just saying that I want to do more. I want to be with her when she's out there fighting, so that I can protect her or something."

Leaf laughed at me, and I can't deny the way that stung. "You can't help her," Leaf said through his laughter. "She's a Gardener. She's built for this. Your empathy, while impressive, won't help you against the kind of monsters she deals with."

I closed my eyes against the feeling of helplessness that welled up within me. It was a feeling that I was intimately familiar with, given my time waiting by Emma's bedside. "I can't keep letting her get hurt," I said, and was horrified by the fact that my voice was choked with tears. "She's all I've got left, Leaf." I opened my eyes and found him blurry. I was crying again.

"How do you think she would feel if you got hurt on her behalf?" Leaf asked. He came closer to me, kneeling by my side once more. I felt him touch my shoulder, then touch my cheek with gentle hands. "She loves you just as much as you love her. I've never seen siblings so devoted to each other."

I leaned forward so that my forehead was resting against his, my breath coming in shuddering gasps. "I need to do something, though. I can't... I can't just keep waiting for the other shoe to drop, Leaf, I can't. If she gets hurt again, goes into a coma again, and it's because I wasn't there to help her, how can I live with that?"

Leaf surged forward and kissed me, his lips soft and warm against my own. I was shocked and I stared at him through wide eyes. He didn't pull away, and I relaxed and leaned into the kiss. It was nice, soft and sweet and everything I'd been wanting for the past few months without having the words for.

"As distractions go," I breathed when he pulled back ever so slightly, "That one was nice."

Leaf laughed, the sound a bit choked. "You'll leave me too, you know. Humans always go." But he continued to stroke my cheek, his fingers soft on my skin.

"I can't do anything about that," I said. "But I can be here with you for awhile at least. Emma and I both can." I reached up and touched his hair. It was soft and clung to my fingers and he tilted his head into the touch. "Help me help her?" I asked.

He sighed. "This is going to go so very poorly," Leaf said. He leaned forward and kissed me again, then pulled back. "I'll help you figure out a plan." He smiled at me, and I smiled back.

I could feel something like hope at the thought of Leaf helping me with Emma, and it was a good feeling. I approved.

"I should probably get back to the hospital," I said with a sigh. "She's gonna be so bored there right now. She hates the channels on the televisions."

"You should probably shower first," Leaf said. He stood and danced back from me, his eyes twinkling. "You humans, you all smell terrible, but right now your bouquet is particularly noticeable."

I flung a handful of fallen leaves at him. "Says the tree who's probably gonna go bald in a few weeks," I shot back. I stood and dusted myself off.

Leaf let out a wounded gasp. "Rude!" He tossed his hair. "I'll have you know that it turns brown, thank you very much."

"So you'll be brown all over?" I asked, then flushed as I realized how my question could be taken. It wasn't what I'd intended, but it was what had apparently come out.

Leaf cleared his throat and glanced away, his own cheeks darkening. "I suppose you'll have to find out eventually," he said. "But not today. Today you need to go visit Emma." Then he was gone, leaving me alone in the yard.

But I didn't feel alone. I could still feel him, soft and warm and steady in my heart, and I went into the house to shower with a smile on my face and a slight spring in my step.

*   *   *

Emma did, in fact, look terribly bored when I entered her hospital room. She was sitting on her bed, staring at the television with a vacant expression on her face that vanished the second I stepped into the room. She made demanding, grabby motions for the laptop case in my hand.

"I see, you only want me for the laptop," I said to her even as I handed it over.

"Please," Emma said with a roll of her eyes. "Don't fish for compliments. You know I'm glad to see you." Then she grinned. "But I'm even happier to see my laptop. Hello, darling." She petted the case. "I've missed you so much."

"It's been less than a day," I protested. "How can you have missed it that much in that short a period of time?"

88

She shook her head at me. "You'll never understand." Then she sobered, green eyes darkening. "So, the cops have been asking me all kinds of questions. A few of them were about you."

I froze and my heart dropped. I'd hoped that they wouldn't seriously think I'd hurt her. "What did you tell them?" I asked. What if they'd thought that I hurt her? What if CPS got involved and took her away?

"I think they were just covering their bases," she said. "I told them that you hadn't hurt me, that you'd never laid a hand on me, and that I hadn't seen any attacker and that all I remembered was falling while I was walking. I think they believed me."

I cleared my throat. Maybe she would confess. "Why wouldn't they believe you? It was the truth, after all."

Emma's lips twitched. "I don't know if you've realized this, but sometimes people don't believe the truth even when it's staring them in the face."

Of course she wouldn't use that opening to tell me. She was going to continue to be stubborn about this. Well. That was fine. I could figure out something anyway. Leaf would help me. Together we might be able to keep her from winding up here again.

Chapter Nine: Cards on the Table

"She's getting out today," I said to Leaf, my voice dull.

"I know," Leaf said. He was sitting at the dining room table with me, his chin resting on the table and his lips tugged into a frown. As he'd told me earlier in the week, his hair was slowly fading to brown. It was strange, and I preferred him with the brighter hair, but it was also nice.

"We haven't thought of anything." I traced the grain of the wood with one finger, staring down at it. A week and we hadn't thought of anything resembling a plan. And Emma was coming home today, which meant that there was every chance that she'd try to go out tonight. Because of course she would.

Leaf sighed. "No," he agreed. "Maybe you should just tell her the truth."

I glanced up at him. He was watching me, his gold eyes almost compassionate. "Tell her that I know what she's been up to? She'll be pissed." And that anger was nothing compared to how furious she'd be when she realized I'd put bars on the window that led to Leaf's tree. He'd watched me do it, laughing the whole time.

One of his eyebrows crept up. "And you don't think you have the right to return the sentiment? She's lied to you as well, after all, and actually managed to get herself hurt. You've only been lying because you didn't want to stress her out."

"But she was only lying because she didn't want to stress..." I stopped. "Okay, no, you're right. We're being idiots. I'm the adult. I'm allowed to be stressed out over my little sister."

Leaf's lips twitched into a smile. "You are," he agreed. "From what I understand, that's common of the older children in families, that they worry about their siblings."

I laughed. "That is my job as her older brother. And I feel like now that I'm her guardian it's even more my job." Then I went back to staring at the grain. "But what if telling her hurts her?"

Leaf let out a noise that I could only describe as a disgusted groan. "Really?" he asked me. I could hear the roll of his eyes in his voice. "She's sixteen. You're her guardian. You can't always be her best friend. If she's angry, then let her be angry. She'll get over it."

I looked up at him. He'd shifted so that his forehead was pressed against the table. "Is that weird for you?" I asked him.

He groaned again, the sound pained. "Is what weird for me?"

I gestured to the table. "Sitting here with the corpse of your fallen brother, discussing how to best help my sister who deals with their angry spirits. Is that weird?"

Leaf shoved away from the table. "You're insane," he said flatly. "I don't know why I like you, you idiot. Go pick your sister up and tell her the fucking truth or I'm just going to ignore both of you until you grow a pair." He stalked out of the room, his wild hair dancing behind him.

"That's awfully crude for a tree spirit, you know!" I called after him. He flipped me off as he left the room. "You're ruining my illusions of you as a prim and proper spirit!"

He didn't say anything, but disappeared just before the door could close. I laughed at him, then took a deep breath. Right. Pick up Emma from the hospital, then sit her down for what would undoubtedly be the most awkward conversation of our lives. I could do that. Honest.

How was I going to start this hypothetical conversation? "Hey, Emma, I know that you're some kind of superhero," I said to myself.

"And stop talking to yourself!" Leaf shouted through the window.

"Stop listening!" I shouted back, then grabbed my keys. I would figure it out on the way to the hospital. That would work.

*   *   *

Emma was bright and bubbly, all smiles and giggles as I wheeled her out of the hospital. "I'm so glad to be getting out of here again," she said to me, her relief obvious. "I've been feeling so caged here. Going home will really be good for me I think."

"I'm sure it will," I agreed. I still hadn't figured out how I was going to start this conversation with her.

"And, I mean, I know you're probably worried that I'm going to start my late night walks again, Jamie, but I promise that I'm not going to." She smiled up at me, her pretty green eyes guileless.

I didn't buy it for a second. "Really?" I drawled, stretching the word out to properly convey my disbelief. There was no way I could make it long enough, but I got the point across. Then I smirked at her. "So you won't mind that I put bars on the windows while you were in the hospital, right? I just wanted to remove the temptation."

"You what?" She twisted in the wheelchair to stare at me, her eyes wide and betrayed. "Jamie, you didn't have to do that! I swear, I'm not going to be going out the window anymore, I just like the view, and with bars there I won't be able to see-"

"The tree?" I asked, cutting her off as we arrived at the car. "You won't be able to see the tree? Because Emma, that's the only view you have from that window."

She swallowed and got into the jeep, her steps not even a bit shaky. She buckled up and waited until I'd started the car and was driving before saying, "I just really like the tree, Jamie, and I really don't want bars on my window."

"Because you're going to keep sneaking out at night." I glanced at her out of the corner of my eye, internally a bit amused to see the way her face screwed up in frustrated rage. I let none of it show.

"Okay, fine, yes because I'm planning on continuing to sneak out at night!" She let out an explosive sigh, full of all the drama that only a high school girl could manage. "But Jamie, you just don't get it!"

I gritted my teeth against the very real anger that surged to life within me. "I don't get it?" I echoed, incredulous. "Please, Emma, explain to me what I don't get. My baby sister, who is now my responsibility, just spent a week in the hospital after sneaking out of the house to do something she won't explain to me. Did you really think there wouldn't be consequences?"

She shook her head. "My getting hurt was just an accident!" She protested, her words tripping over each other as they fell from her lips. "I wasn't being careful, Jamie, but it's not something that will happen again! I'll be super careful next time and I won't get hurt and everything will be fine. You just have to take the bars off the window!"

"You'll be careful next time and it won't happen again." I shook my head. "Emma, they're called accidents for a reason. We don't plan them, they just happen. Or do you think that Mom and Dad-"

"This isn't like that!" Emma let out a frustrated groan. "You're just... you're not my father, James, and you can't tell me what to do!"

"I'm sorry, but the law says that's pretty much what I am!" Then I winced. I hadn't meant to say that.

"Well the law is bullshit!" Emma shouted back.

"Okay, you know what?" I asked, keeping my voice as even as I could. It wasn't easy. "Why don't we drive the rest of the way in silence and we can both think over what we want to say about this. Then we can talk about it at home." With Leaf there to make sure I didn't give up and strangle her, because I was honestly considering it.

"Fine." She sank back into the chair, her arms crossed, a scowl fixed on her face. She was furious, but so was I.

The rest of the drive passed in stony silence, with my eyes fixed on the road ahead. She meant everything to me, but she didn't care about that. She didn't care about her own safety. She wanted to keep doing this thing, saving these plants or whatever, because… why? Why was this so important to her?

I chanced a glance at her as we pulled into the driveway. She was wiping angrily at her eyes and my heart dropped. "Jesus, don't cry Emma," I asked her.

"How can I not cry?" she asked me. "You don't trust me. Do you think I'm doing something illegal?"

"Oh for fuck's sake," Leaf said, popping into existence beside us. "He knows exactly what you're doing, you nitwit. And by the way, thanks for getting your ass kicked and making me call 911 on your phone. That was just the most fun I've ever had in my life."

"Leaf!" Emma's tears vanished like they'd never been and she stared at him, betrayal clear in her eyes. "You told him what I was doing?"

"Told him what you were doing?" Leaf laughed. "Please. He followed you one night."

Emma whirled on me, her eyes sparking. "You followed me? You didn't trust me, Jamie?"

"Oh for-" I cut off and took a deep breath. I locked the car, then started into the house. "No, Emma, I didn't trust you. You were sneaking out behind my back constantly. You wouldn't tell me where you were going, what you were doing, or who you were doing it with. It was a nightmare. So yes, I followed you."

96

"You let him?" she asked Leaf.

Leaf stared at her, his most unimpressed look on his face. "Listen here, little girl. I don't stop humans from making stupid mistakes. I tried with you and you saw, and felt, how well that worked out for you. Why would I have stopped your brother from following you?"

Emma sat down at the table with a huff. "How long have you known?" she asked me.

I shrugged. "A few months," I said to her. "Since late September."

"And you didn't tell me?" Her indignance would have had more weight if it weren't for the fact that she'd been keeping some pretty big secrets from me as well.

"You're some kind of superhero and you didn't think that was something I needed to know?" I shot back at her.

She flushed. "You've been so stressed lately. I just didn't want to add to your burden." Then her eyes narrowed. "And it's superheroine, thank you very much."

I stared at her. "Let me tell you something, sister mine, knowing that your sister is sneaking out of the house but not knowing what she's up to is infinitely more stressful than knowing that you're dealing with the angry spirits of plants." Then I thought over what I'd just said. "Though, honestly, I kind of wish you weren't doing that either."

"Well I'm not going to stop," she said, her chin lifted in defiance. "So you might as well take the bars off the window because I'm going out there one way or another. I'm doing good things, Jamie. I'm helping people!"

"Never said you weren't, and I never said you had to stop." I smiled at her. "I'm going to start going with you."

She shook her head. "No," she said immediately. "It's too dangerous. You'll be hurt."

"Oh, like you were?" I raised an eyebrow at her in challenge and she stared back at me, her mouth gaping open. "That's right. I had to sit in a hospital for you again. Do you know how hard that was for me? So I'm going with you now."

"No, I-" She stopped and took a deep breath. "Leaf, tell him that he can't. Tell him that it's too dangerous, and that he'll be hurt if he tries to go with me."

Leaf shrugged. "It's not like he doesn't know the dangers. Your brother's been working with some of the plants himself."

She turned back to me. "You've what?" she asked, her voice shrill with surprise.

"I've been helping some of them," I said with a shrug. "Soothing them so that they didn't turn into problems that you'd have to deal with later. Turns out I'm some kind of empath."

"Some kind of..." She stopped, took a deep breath, then said severely, "Jamie, that's very dangerous. I don't want you to keep doing that."

I raised an eyebrow at her, waited to see if she was serious. When she stared at me evenly, I let out a loud laugh. "Emma, you know, it's funny, but I've been thinking that what you're doing is terribly dangerous and I don't want you to keep doing that."

"That's different!" she protested.

I stared at her, my eyebrows raised. "Is it?" I asked. "Because I do agree, actually. It is different. I'm older than you and I'm allowed to make stupid decisions about my life. I'm an adult. You're not. You're my ward. You're not allowed to make dangerous decisions like that."

"That's not fair!" I swear, Emma was about a second away from stomping her foot.

"Life isn't," Leaf interjected. "If it were fair, your parents would still be here and you would never have awoken as a Gardener."

I shot him a grateful look. "Look, Ems, I'm not saying that you can't do this anymore at all. I wouldn't say that. I'm just saying that I want to be there when you do."

Emma glared at me, the force of it strong enough for me to almost feel the weight of it. "You'll get hurt," she said finally. "I don't want you to be hurt."

"I don't care if I get hurt," I said to her. "It's my job to get hurt so that you don't have to."

"That's a stupid job," she muttered. She looked down at the table, then looked back up at me. "Fine. You can come with me when I go out, but if you get hurt I reserve the right to tell you that I told you so."

"Noted," I said, my lips quirking into a smile.

"And Leaf, I'm pissed at you, okay? How dare you tell him what I was doing." She glared at the tree spirit.

Leaf raised one eyebrow at her. "Oh dear. A teenager, angry with me. However shall I survive?"

She tossed her hair and stood. "Now, if you'll excuse me, I'm going to go to my room and catch up on some of my homework, since I'd like to be back at school on Monday."

"Have fun!" I said.

She didn't answer, but disappeared upstairs. Moments after she did so, I heard her let out an outraged shriek. "Jamie, you asshole!" she shouted.

"What?" I asked. "I didn't do anything!"

"You really did put bars on my window!"

I couldn't help it, my laughter exploded from me and I heard the windows rattle with the force of her door slamming. I laughed so hard that tears rolled down my cheeks and Leaf came over to check and see if I was okay by resting his hands on my shoulders.

"Calm down. I don't want to have to call an ambulance again just because you couldn't stop laughing," Leaf said dryly.

That set me off again and he sighed. "Humans," he muttered, but stayed by my side rather than disappearing.

Chapter Ten - Working Together

Once I'd calmed down, I found myself staring at Leaf, who was looking back at me with an eyebrow raised. "What?" Leaf asked, his eyebrow creeping further up.

"We kissed," I said. Then I cleared my throat and flushed. "We, umm, well." I cleared my throat again and stared down at the table. I was getting far too familiar with the grain of its wood. It was a nice table. A great table, in fact, that had been in my family for generations.

"Oh for fuck's sake, stop staring at the damn table," Leaf said. I heard him move, and then he was tilting my head up and kissing me again. My eyes fluttered shut and I leaned into it. My eyes stayed closed when he pulled away, and I rested my head against his stomach. "You're ridiculous," Leaf said, but he said it fondly.

"I don't mean to be," I said. I could feel him breathing, slow and steady. I could feel his affection for me, deep and welling up from nowhere. It was wonderful. "You have to know that I've never really done the whole relationship thing." Then I thought about Maya and winced.

"Successfully, I mean. I've never done the relationship thing successfully."

"Relationship thing?" Leaf echoed, laughter warming his voice.

I tensed and jerked back. "If we're in a relationship, I mean." I didn't look up at him. "I never meant to imply that-"

"Are all humans so stupid?" Leaf asked, cutting me off. He tilted my head up again. "We're in a relationship. Even though you'll eventually die and leave me, if you don't get tired of me before then, we're in a relationship." Then he smirked at me. "And I can assure you, I'm good enough at this 'relationship thing' for both of us."

I breathed out in relief. "Thank you," I said to him, my voice shaky. "I don't really know how I'd do this without you."

"You wouldn't," Leaf said, then leaned down and kissed me again. I sighed into it and let my eyes close. "You seem tired," Leaf murmured.

"It's been a long few days," I said to him. He felt warm and steady and wonderful, and given the chaos of the past few days it was an incredibly nice feeling.

"You should get some rest. You'll probably sleep easier now that Emma's out of the hospital." Leaf ran a hand through my hair and I tilted my head into the touch.

"That sounds like a good idea," I said, because even though it was the middle of the day I found myself pretty exhausted. Then, hesitantly, I asked, "Stay?" My voice shook a bit, but I managed to get the word out.

"If you'd like," Leaf said. He tugged me to my feet and started up the stairs ahead of me.

I hesitated inside of my bedroom. "Just to sleep," I said quickly, before I lost my nerve. "I don't... I don't want to do anything else."

"That sounds nice," Leaf said. He was watching me, confusion in his golden eyes and pushing at the edges of my consciousness. "Whatever you'd like is fine with me."

I took a deep breath and let it out slowly. "And if I don't ever want to do more than we've done?" I asked. It wasn't something I liked talking about and was definitely the reason I'd never really tried dating aside from Maya. The conversation was almost always guaranteed to be an awkward one, though it was slowly becoming less so as society grew more accepting.

"I don't know if you've realized this," Leaf said, his voice dry. "But I'm a tree spirit. Sex isn't necessarily something I'm terribly interested in. I don't exactly have the right parts for that sort of thing anyway."

I could feel his sincerity. I relaxed and felt my legs go weak with relief and a sudden wave of exhaustion. Leaf caught me before I could hit the ground. "If I'd known you were so worried about this I would have said something sooner." He helped me over to the bed and I sat down with a heavy thump.

I took a few deep breaths and smiled at him, but the expression was a bit shaky. "I didn't realize that I was so worried about it," I told him. Well. I'd known I was worried, but I hadn't realized I was that worried. Hadn't realized how attached I was already. How much my heart would have broken if that had been a dealbreaker.

I guess reading other people's emotions didn't help put me more in touch with my own. Good to know.

"You've had too much on your mind these past few days," Leaf said. Then he was kneeling at my feet and taking off my shoes for me. "And I know you haven't been sleeping well. You need to tell me when you're so stressed. Empaths always feel negative emotions so much more strongly."

"Yeah?" I asked, staring down at him. My shoes were off, then, and I brought my legs up to stretch out on the bed.

"Yeah," Leaf said. I felt the bed dip and then he was curled around me, his head resting on the pillow next to my own. "It's not good for you to get yourself all worked up like this."

"I'll try to keep that in mind," I said to him, my words slurring a bit with my exhaustion.

"You should," Leaf said, soft and sweet in my ear. "I don't want you to get to the point you were at after helping your first spirit."

"It's sweet that you're worried about me," I murmured.

He pressed a soft kiss to my cheek and nestled closer to me, blanketing me in both physical and mental warmth. "I like worrying about you. Which is good, because humans are foolish and I feel like worrying about you is all that I'll ever do."

I wanted to object and opened my mouth to do so, but the words wouldn't come. So instead I just let out a tiny, protesting hum and he laughed at me. Then my eyes were drifting closed and I was asleep.

*   *   *

A week later and I was finally ready to let Emma go out again. She'd been relatively good natured about my restrictions, meaning that she only bitched at me at most twice a day about my choosing not to let her go outside. Well. I let her go outside, but I wouldn't let her out of the house past ten and she'd been good enough about respecting my wishes.

Well. By good enough about respecting my wishes, I meant that she'd only tried to sneak past me three times, and all three times hadn't tried again in the same night.

"C'mon, c'mon, c'mon!" She was almost dancing in place, her left foot tapping restlessly and her arms swinging back and forth. It was clear that she was excited.

"I don't get why you're so happy for this," I said, even as I grabbed my keys and threw on a coat. It was cold out and I didn't want to wander around the alleys and get frostbite. "Also, where's your coat?" Speaking of frostbite...

She rolled her eyes in the way that only a teenage girl could manage. "Jamie. Big brother. I'm going to be running around. I don't need a coat because I'll be working up a sweat."

I stared at her until she sighed and, with another theatrical eye roll, grabbed her coat. "I'm not wearing it when we get to the site."

"That's fine," I said, and unlocked the door. She was out in a flash and halfway down the block before I reached the car. I unlocked it and the beep drew her attention.

"Jamie! What do you need from the car?" she asked, exasperation clear in her tone.

I grinned at her. "I mean, if you want to walk that's fine, but Leaf says that we're going about two miles away and I thought the car would be a good idea, especially if either of us get injured."

"Huh." She cocked her head to one side, then she grinned. "Well then. I knew there would be some kind of benefit to allowing you to come with me."

Like I'd given her much of a choice. Still, I could be gracious in victory. To a point. I opened the door and sat in the car and waited until she'd opened the passenger side before saying, "Leaf already called shotgun."

Emma's expression was priceless. "What, seriously?" she protested, even as Leaf appeared in the car next to me. "Fine, whatever." Her third eye roll was audible more than visible, but she climbed into the back seat without any argument.

"So. Exact location of our target?" I asked, even as I turned the car on.

"It's not exactly a precise science, you know," Emma complained.

"But you should start heading in the direction of the hospital," Leaf said. He looked behind himself and shot a dirty look in Emma's direction. "Emma or I will tell you when you need to turn off of the main road."

The drive was silent for all of a minute before Emma burst out with, "So what was it like working with Leaf for you, Jamie? Is he as overbearing to you as he is to me?"

I laughed and shook my head. "It was nice, working with him. I'm pretty sure he saved my life, you know."

"I knew this was too dangerous for you," Emma said immediately. "We should turn around and you should stay in the house. I'll be fine, Jamie."

"It's not…" I sighed. "You remember the day that I was really depressed, right?"

"Yeah," Emma said. "I was worried about you. I'd never seen you like that before."

"It was after he worked with a tree that was dying. If left alone, it would have turned into a spirit for you to deal with later," Leaf said. He was leaning back in the seat, his eyes closed. "Turn left here, by the way." As I turned, he continued with, "I miscalculated the amount of depression that feeling the plant's death would cause in your brother, and it might have driven him to suicide if I hadn't realized what had happened. Now that we know, it hasn't happened since."

"It helps that there haven't been any dying spirits lately," I said thoughtfully as I drove down a small residential road.

"None that I've taken you to," Leaf muttered. "And Emma, if you notice him acting like that again, I need you to come get me immediately. It shouldn't happen again, but if it does I need your word."

I shot him a look, but he said nothing.

"I'm glad you were able to help him," Emma said. "And of course you have my word. He's my brother, you know. I don't want him to get hurt." She took a deep breath and let it out slowly. Then, with a soft gasp, she said, "Do you feel that? Turn right here!"

I did feel it, and I didn't particularly want to turn right. But I did, and the sense of decay and wrongness got stronger as I drove down the alley. It was only a couple of feet before I saw it. It was massive and wrong and sick and dark and disgusting, and it looked to be terrorizing a german shepherd in one of the yards. "That looks awful," I said, and my voice barely came out.

Emma's scoff was audible. "Please," she said. She clambered out of the car and shouted to get the thing's attention, and I hoped that she didn't get anyone else's attention while she was at it.

When the thing lunged for her she danced out of its way, then danced back further, her body starting to glow green as she whispered those strange words again, her fingers dancing. Leaf was standing there, just watching, and didn't even twitch when the thing got her around the ankle and threw her.

"Emma!" I shouted, and rushed to her side. She was already getting back up, dusting herself off. "Are you okay?"

"Please, I'm fine," she said, then shrieked when she was thrown again.

"Right, you're fine," I said. I jumped between her and the monster and immediately regretted it when the thing threw me too. "Ow," I muttered as I landed on the asphalt, my vision going a bit blurry from the force of my landing.

"Hey, leave my brother alone!" Emma shouted, followed by more nonsense words that made no sense to me. Then there was a flash of green light and the monster was gone and Emma was at my side, helping me to my feet. "You idiot," she said to me as she dusted me off. "This is why I didn't want you to come! You could have been killed, and then what would I have done?"

"I'm fine," I said. I grabbed her hands and stilled them. "Really. Don't worry about me, please."

"He's too hardheaded to have actually been injured by that," Leaf interjected, a smirk on his lips.

"Thanks, I think," I said to him. Then I slung an arm around Emma's shoulder. "But hey, you got thrown around a few times too. You okay?"

"That?" Emma blinked up at me. "That was nothing. I get thrown around like that all the time. I'm fine."

"That was nothing?" I echoed. If that had been nothing, what had happened to land her in the hospital? Suddenly, I really didn't want to know. "Right. That was nothing." I laughed, a bit nervously.

"She's fine," Leaf said, appearing beside me. His hand rested on my shoulder, a steadying presence, and I relaxed a bit. "You're fine too. Relax. Stop panicking."

"I'm not panicking!" I protested, then winced. Maybe I was a bit panicky, but who wouldn't be?

"Course you're not!" Emma said. She wrapped an arm around my waist and started tugging me towards the car. "We're both fine. Leaf is fine. Everything is fine."

I took a deep breath, slung an arm around Leaf's shoulder to drag him with us, and said, "You're right. Everything is fine."

It wasn't quite. I felt like there was still a lot to work out, and I was sure that Emma wouldn't deal with my restrictions forever as gracefully as she'd dealt this week, but for the first time since I'd had custody of Emma, I was certain of one thing:

We could work this out, and everything would be fine.

Epilogue

Two years had passed, Emma was eighteen now, and things were going well. She was just starting her senior year of high school and, in spite of the fact that she no longer needed to listen to me, she tended to do so anyway. She still abided by my restrictions and she still took me along with her even though she didn't have to. Sometimes I got beat up, but she wasn't too mean about it.

"Are you even listening to me?" Leaf was glaring at me when I snapped my eyes over to meet his. He was standing by the newest sapling in the greenhouse, his hands carefully stroking one of its leaves. No spirit had manifested yet, but considering that the little guy wasn't even a year old, I wasn't surprised. He'd show up eventually.

"Of course I am," I said with a grin. "You were talking about your fear that he won't grow up, and your worry that you did something wrong. You didn't. It'll be fine." I knew it would.

"You don't know that," Leaf said, stroking the leaves with gentle fingers. "How could you know that?"

Because I could feel it. I could feel the sapling's contentedness, a soft sleepy feeling that told me there was definitely a spirit growing in there. The feelings grew with every day. Everything in the greenhouse had those sorts of feelings, but most of them were barely there.

Of course, I'd told him that fifty times. Still, one more time wouldn't hurt. "Because I can feel it," I said aloud.

Leaf sighed. "You're sure that you're feeling him and not one of the other trees?" Leaf asked.

There was a soft giggle, echoed by hundreds of other giggles from the tiny saplings and baby bushes that surrounded us. I could feel the joy of the flowers, the pleasure of the ones getting watered right at that moment by the automated sprinkler system. It was wonderful. Leaf's idea had been the best idea ever, actually.

Even if he was a paranoid worrier. "Am I ever wrong about who's feeling what feeling these days?" I asked with fond exasperation. Maybe when I'd been newer to all of this, maybe there had been a few embarrassing mishaps, but that had been a long time ago. I didn't make mistakes anymore.

"If you're sure," Leaf said. He stepped away from the sapling and crossed the room to me. He looped his arms around my waist and kissed me.

I let my eyes flutter closed and leaned into his kiss. I never got tired of that. Never got tired of him. Sometimes I still worried that he'd get tired of me, that he'd leave me one day because I was just a foolish human, but it hadn't happened yet.

"Hey, Leaf, how's your sapling grow- Oh. My. God."

I froze, and Leaf did too. I could feel Emma's shock, battering against me like a ram. I jerked away from Leaf and turned to Emma, my mind racing for an explanation. "Hey, Ems, this really isn't-"

She was grinning at me, her hands clasped beneath her chin, her eyes wide with glee and a bit of hope. "Oh my god, please tell me that the two of you are dating," she breathed.

I cleared my throat. "Um. Sort of?" I hazarded. Leaf stepped up beside me and curled his hand around my own.

"We are," he said, as unflappable as he almost always was. When he wasn't worrying about his sapling.

"Since when?" she asked, her voice going higher.

"Um. Two years?" I tried. I winced and closed my eyes under the anticipated onslaught of irritation that I'd kept it from her.

Instead I got a flare of the brightest joy I'd ever felt from my sister. "Oh my god! Two years, seriously? I'm so happy for you!" She lunged forward and wrapped her arms around us both, squeezing tightly. "Is that..." She stopped, her eyes widening, and then she turned and stared at the sapling, planted in the dirt in the center of the greenhouse, unlike the others which lived in pots until they were sold.

"No," Leaf said quickly. "It's not what you're thinking."

"You're raising a child together," she breathed.

I groaned. "No, Emma," I said. Even though I wasn't entirely certain she was wrong.

"Yes!" she squealed, and punched the air. "You know, I was wondering if you'd ever give me a niece or nephew," she said. "I mean, sure, he or she won't be the most traditional niece or nephew, but whatever. I'm going to spoil this sweet thing, yes I am." Now she was cooing at the tree, giggling intermittently.

"I don't-" Leaf stopped himself and sighed. "She won't listen, will she?" he asked me.

"I'm not entirely sure that she's wrong," I told him, my lips twitching. "We are going to raise him together. Or her."

"Yeah," Leaf said. "I guess you're right."

Emma had now pulled out a bottle of water with a blue label and was pouring some of it into the dirt surrounding Leaf's sapling. "Is this the kind you'll like too? Your mother likes this kind the best."

"I am not the mother!" Leaf burst out, and lunged for Emma, who ducked away laughing.

This was my life now. Our life, and it was probably the best life I could have wound up with. It wasn't perfect, but no life was, and I think it would have been boring if it had been.

I heard something clatter to the ground further in the greenhouse, likely an empty pot or something, and laughing, I went to stop the carnage. This was a good life.

Want more?

Check out the first chapter of *Devotee of War* by Robin Blackwell, now available for Kindle and in paperback.

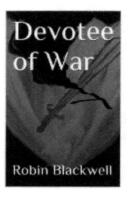

When Seren turned twenty, he was branded a failure for all the world to see.

Cast out from society, friendless and penniless, every day is a struggle for Seren to survive and few are interested in helping him. Half-starved and barely holding on, Seren waits for the coming of winter which will surely claim his life. When the first snowstorm of the year hits, Seren sits, ready to die, when he hears a child crying out for help.

Seren's attempt to help the child changes his fate and brings him to the god he worshiped from afar, who, as it happens, was always rather intrigued by him.

Chapter One-

The blades clashed as Seren brought his sword up just in time to block the blow. He felt a flash of pride at the success which was immediately followed by a flash of pain in his side and then blackness.

He blinked open his bright green eyes to find himself staring at the painfully familiar grey ceiling of Nyara's Temple, more commonly known as the infirmary.

"Oh for fuck's sake," Seren muttered, and tried to sit up. The world spun around him and he immediately stopped moving, staying on his back. He didn't want to see how pale he'd gone just then, considering how pale he already was.

"Back again?"

Seren turned his head just slightly to glare at the attendant. An Acolyte of Nyara, goddess of medicine, stood watching him. The same Acolyte that was always his attendant when he wound up in the infirmary, actually. Ishan was his name, and while he was always careful to take care of Seren, he wasn't exactly known for his bedside manner.

"You don't need to sound so unsurprised," Seren said.

"I'm not surprised," Ishan said. He crossed the room and settled at Seren's side. "Nobody's surprised. Yerin wasn't surprised when he got you. Battlemaster Havarel wasn't surprised when Yerin told him he'd knocked you unconscious. Healer Toreia wasn't surprised when you were

120

brought in on the stretcher they'd had set aside for you. Absolutely nobody was surprised."

Seren groaned and covered his eyes with his arm, trapping a few wayward strands of his long brown hair. "I was really trying, too," he said. It was hard to get the words out around the lump that was rising in his throat.

"Yerin said that you actually managed to block him, so that was something like an improvement, right?" Ishan patted his shoulder with something like sympathy. "Yerin was going at half-strength, because he didn't actually want to hurt you, but you did block him. So maybe..."

Seren swallowed around the lump that was now firmly lodged. "That was nice of him," he said. He was glad that he'd covered his eyes because Ishan wouldn't hesitate to mock him relentlessly should he catch him crying. Then again, considering what today was, he probably would let Seren cry without any mocking.

"It was. If he hadn't been pulling his blows you would probably probably have been a full week recovering. As it stands, you should be okay soon. You might even be able to stand without having the room spinning too much in the next few minutes." Seren heard the chair creak and knew that Ishan had stood. "Did you want to try now?"

"I just did and it didn't work," Seren said. "Why is my head injured, anyway? I'm pretty sure I got hit in the side."

"You did," Ishan said quietly. "But you also hit your head when you went down, and that's what we're mostly concerned with. Head wounds are… tricky, and you've had more than your fair share of them."

Seren wrinkled his nose, but didn't argue the point. He said nothing for several minutes, waiting until he felt like he could talk without crying. It took longer than he wanted to admit, but eventually his breath stopped hitching and the wetness in his eyes dried.

"I guess I could try again," he said, and removed his hand from his eyes.

Ishan was staring at him, dispassionate. "Ready to catch you when you fall," the Acolyte of Nyara said.

"Because that's comforting," Seren said. Then, carefully, he sat up. The room spun, but not as badly as it had moments ago. His breath left him in a heavy sigh. "Great, I'm up." He raked his hands through his hair and tried to calm it into some semblance of order.

"You're sitting," Ishan corrected. "Now try standing, and if you can walk to the entrance to the infirmary without my help then you're free to go."

Seren sighed. He didn't exactly want to rush leaving the infirmary. "Right," he said, then carefully placed his bare feet on the cold stone of the infirmary. His armor had been removed and he was wearing the pale grey shift that all Devotees and Acolytes of Firien wore when they weren't in active training. While it was more comfortable than the armor, it did nothing for the chill in the temple.

He stood, his legs a bit shakier than he liked. Ishan stood very close to him, no doubt prepared to catch him should he falter. Really, if he were more clever, Seren would wait until he was feeling much better to try to make the walk out of the temple. Then again, nobody ever accused him of being clever.

He took his first step, and didn't fall. He took one more, a bit shaky still, then another. The shakiness lessened with every step he took and finally he was standing at the entrance to the temple. "Well. Guess I'm good to go, right?" he asked Ishan. He had to swallow and blink rapidly against the tears that wanted to fall at the thought.

Ishan stared at him, then handed him a pair of soft slippers. "Wear these on your way back to the temple of Firien so that you don't stub your toe and wind up back in here," Ishan said. He looked down and didn't look back up when he said, "Also, Havarel would like to see you in his office."

"Of course he would," Seren said. The lump was coming back to his throat and his rapid blinking wasn't really doing much to stave off the tears that were starting to escape his eyes. Havarel needed to see him. Of course he did. And Seren knew exactly what conversation would follow.

He toed on the slippers and left the temple of Nyara, stepping out in the bright sunlight. It was a beautiful day, cloudless and neither too warm nor too cold. It was perfect weather, and all around him Devotees and Acolytes wandered through the immaculate grounds of the Academy. Of course it was a beautiful day, and of course it was crowded.

Seren gritted his teeth, scrubbed roughly at his eyes, and started the long walk back to Firien's temple. He wondered how many of these Acolytes and Devotees had seen him be carried through, unconscious, on the stretcher. It didn't matter, and he tried to brush the thought off. The snickers and whispers that sprung up in his wake didn't help him, and by the end of his walk he was blinking back more tears.

He needed to calm down before facing Havarel or the conversation would be more awful than it was already going to be. Seren took several deep breaths, then stepped into the temple itself. The first room was the Shrine of Firien, a cavernous room with an empty and plain iron throne at the center of it on a raised dais. In front of the throne on the first step down was a padded carpet for kneeling, so that supplicants could offer Firien their prayers in something like comfort. Off to either side were the long tables for the offerings, which were currently rather empty. One of the Battlemasters must have gone through and cleared them moments ago, because there were still several supplicants kneeling. In the center of the room was the Fire of War, which blazed eternal as humans had yet to find true peace.

It was there that Seren went. He grabbed a candle from one of the small baskets by the door and lit it from the Fire of War. Then, lit candle held reverently with both hands, Seren went to kneel before the throne of his god.

My lord Firien, he thought, his lips moving soundlessly. It's Seren. I'm so sorry to bother you, and I know that I must be a bother because you never answer my prayers. Or maybe you do, and that block that I managed today was your doing. In which case, thank you. I appreciate it. It might be enough... who am I kidding? It's not enough. I am not enough.

Seren took a deep breath and focused on the flame in front of him, letting the breath out with a shuddering sigh.

I did try, though, my lord, and I hope that you can see that. Not that I think you have any time for me, but I really did try my best. I hope that you appreciated my efforts. I don't know, maybe they made you laugh. I guess that would have made this all worth it.

The flame on the candle went out, then, despite the fact that Seren hadn't felt a breeze. He stared at it for a long minute, then sighed and stood. Even his god didn't want to hear it from him today.

Thanks for your time.

Seren left the shrine with steps that were shaky again, but for an entirely different reason than earlier. Battlemaster Havarel was waiting for him, and putting it off would do no good. It was best to just get the conversation over with.

He found the Battlemaster's office and took a deep breath before tapping on the door.

"Enter!" Havarel called sharply.

Seren slipped into the room, closed the door behind him, then flowed to his knees, his hands folded in his lap. "You asked to see me, Battlemaster Havarel?"

"Get up Seren," Havarel said. Seren didn't argue, but stood immediately. He kept his head lowered. "Sit down. In the chair, please."

Seren chanced a glance at Havarel's face. The Battlemaster looked old and tired. His grey eyes were dull and what remained of his silver hair was mussed, as though he'd been raking his fingers through it. There was no paperwork on the desk before him, a rarity for the Battlemaster who ran the Academy of War.

He looked defeated, and Seren's heart dropped. He sat in the chair, not because he wanted to but because his legs would no longer support him. "Battlemaster, I-"

"Shut up," Havarel said.

Seren's mouth closed with a small snap.

"You have to know that I don't entirely agree with this, Seren," Havarel started.

Seren closed his eyes. "Of course, Battlemaster," Seren whispered. He couldn't speak any louder. He could barely manage to get those words out. He'd known, but a small part of him had still hoped...

"But I also don't entirely disagree with this. Seren, in all of my years at the Academy, I've never found someone less suited to the paths of War than you."

Seren flinched. "I managed that block today, so I-"

"You know that wasn't enough, and that isn't even what I'm talking about," Havarel said, not without gentleness. "Were you not a warrior, that would be one thing. There is still a place among the Battlemasters for strategists, for tacticians, even for message bearers. But you've shown no aptitude for anything of the sort, Seren. You can't run without tripping, you can't win a game of strategy, and you can't direct others. You can't block a clearly telegraphed blow without months of training."

Each word of the litany hit Seren like a blow. It was all true, of course. "I'm sorry I'm such a disappointment," he managed to whisper. He stared down at his hands and tried to fight back the tears that were coming. He lost that battle, too, and his tears dripped down onto his hands.

"I'm sorry too," Havarel said. Seren heard the scrape of his chair. "You know that you're very beautiful, so it wasn't particularly difficult to find a placement for you with Madame Rimer. You certainly won't command the most glamorous of clients, and you won't make much money, but it's the best option for you."

"I won't go to a brothel," Seren bit out, though his voice trembled.

"Don't be foolish, Seren," Havarel snapped. "You know what's coming, and you know as well as I what happens to failed Devotees."

"I'd rather be on the streets than be a whore, especially to the type of people that would pay to fuck a Brand," Seren said. He wiped at his eyes, then, and looked up. Havarel was standing near the fireplace, staring at him. "At least if I'm on the streets I'm not bringing more shame to my family. I think I've done enough of that, don't you?"

"There is no shame in-"

"Don't be stupid," Seren said, bitterness leaking into his words. "There's nothing but shame in this, no matter what path I take. If I go to Rimer then all of the nobles will talk about it. If I disappear then they may know, but they'll never be able to prove it."

Havarel nodded once, sharply. "I understand," he said, and Seren might be mistaken but there was a hint of approval in those dull eyes of his. He cleared his throat. "Seren, will you kneel for me?" he asked, a definitive formality in his tone.

Seren closed his eyes and took a deep breath. "I will, Battlemaster Havarel." He was proud that his voice didn't waver. He came out of the chair and dropped his knees with practiced ease.

"Seren, will you give me your hands?" Havarel asked, still with the strict rigor of the ritual in his voice.

Seren immediately extended his hands, palms down. This was what he deserved for failing, and he would shame neither himself nor his god with reluctance. "I will," he said, as his hands were slid into a curious device, a stone surface that his palms rested flat against while cold iron manacles locked around his wrists, holding him in place.

"Seren, will you submit to bear the sign of your failure so that the world might know of your shame?" Havarel's voice broke a bit on the last word and Seren was almost comforted to know that he truly regretted this.

"I will," he said, and bowed so that his bound hands were extended flat on the floor before him and his forehead was flat against the ground. He felt weights settle and knew that the stone holder had been locked into place. He couldn't have fought now if he'd ever intended to.

He took a deep breath and held it and the pain of the first brand touching his right hand made him lose it all in a scream. There was no shame in screaming, but he did what he could to hold still. He managed for the first. The second wasn't as easy, and he couldn't help but flinch from the blinding pain of the iron on his left hand.

Then it was over and the iron was being pulled away, the scent of his cooked flesh strong in the room. Seren barely had time to catch his breath before Havarel was speaking once more.

"You have been with us for twenty summers, Devotee Seren of the House of War, and you have failed to find a way to serve your god in a manner that is appropriate," Havarel said as he carefully smeared a cool cream over the raw burns. "Though it grieves us to do so, we find that we must cast you from our House, that we may have room for new blood who may find the purpose that you lack." Havarel unshackled him, then wrapped his hands in clean gauze. "We name you now Seren of no house, and banish you from the Academy, effective immediately."

At this point Havarel should have stepped away from him and turned his back on him. Instead, he said quietly, "There is a temple of Nyara in the eastern slums of Valgard. They will treat anyone, regardless of their circumstances. If your brands become infected, swear that you'll go to them, Seren."

"I will," Seren whispered, his voice clogged with the tears that he couldn't stop from falling.

"Good boy," Havarel said. He tugged Seren to his feet and then in for a rough hug, and Seren felt something land in his right pocket. "Take care of yourself, Seren. As best you can. May Mercy, if such a deity exists, look out for you."

Then Havarel was pulling away and turning his back to him, and Seren stared at the back of the man who had all but raised him. "I'm sorry to have been such a disappointment," Seren whispered, and Havarel didn't respond.

Seren was dead to him now.

He left the room and found several of the younger Devotees waiting outside of the door. They saw him, and their eyes widened. Immediately, every single one of them turned their backs on him.

Seren took a deep breath and started walking, his head held high. Now, instead of whispers, silence fell in his wake. Every person he met took immediate notice of the bandages on his hands and turned their back on him without so much as a word. It hurt, to be dead to people that he'd grown up with, but Seren said nothing because he was no longer a person.

He was a failure, and now the world would know it.

He reached the gate to the Academy and turned back to look, but his vision was too blurry to really see anything at all. Seren took a deep breath and, for the first time in his memory, stepped outside into the city of Valgard without an escort. He wasn't leaving the way he'd planned when he was younger. He wasn't a Battlemaster, or even a messenger or scout. He was nothing, and the brands on his hands would make sure that everyone knew it.

There was a whole world waiting for him, and all of it would hate him.

Interested in keeping up with Robin Blackwell?

Check her out on Tumblr at Robinblackwellwrites. She posts monthly newsletters, snippets of writing, and the occasional rant about the writing process. She also posts whenever a new story is published. She would love to hear from her fans, and hopes to hear from you soon!

CPSIA information can be obtained
at www.ICGtesting.com
Printed in the USA
LVHW080056230221
679685LV00017B/2684